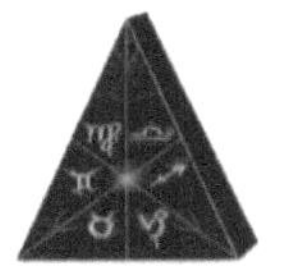

Something Lost

Sarah Dale

For Erin Willis

Printed in the United States of America

This edition Printed, 2020

ISBN-13: 978-1-948661-88-1
AISN: 978-1-948661-87-4

If you're reading this, you've found my hidey hole I've been keeping journals of our adventures for more than three decades now, and up until last week, I believed them to be safely hidden in my home. Now, everything has changed.

It's not that I fear they will be discovered, rather the opposite; I fear they'll be destroyed, and the record of our life's work would simply disappear.

I'm putting them here for safekeeping. I've spent enough hours in this library to know what gets tended regularly, and what gets regularly overlooked. So if you're finding this now, you must be doing a deep clean, or maybe, just maybe, the City has come together with the funds for a new building, and this one is being cleared out.

Do me a favor. Do what you can to keep these safe. Tuck them back away, or move them if you need to, but don't let them be destroyed.

And if it's you they're meant for, then, good luck, my friend. You're going to need it.

"You're Angie Parsons, right?" Barb asked in a low, tight voice. She was tall, nearly as tall as Jen. Her hair was long and black, and stick straight. I nodded quickly in response. "You're one of the kids that fought Charlie's ghost on Halloween." She pinned me with a laser-stare. "That was you, right?"

I first met Barb and Crystal in the spring of 1985 in Social Studies class. They showed up midway through our 8th-grade year, looking out of place, sitting as far in the back as Ms. Jackson would permit.

I'd heard other kids say they were *Whitehall Kids*. Whitehall was the neighborhood group home for troubled children. Mostly they went to their own school, right there on the campus where the Whitehall Mansion was located. But sometimes, some came to public school for a little while. I'd heard stories that the kids there were criminals, or did drugs, or were runaways. But those rumors never came with any specifics, or explanations of why any of them had done those things.

I was fascinated by Barb. She was everything I wasn't. She was tough and dark and dangerous looking. Boys stepped out of her way in the hall. I either got ignored or walked into, like I was invisible. I felt pretty confident in my strengths, more so now than a few years ago for sure, but it would have been nice to look the part. And she certainly did.

Crystal was the more delicate, more skittish of the two, but that didn't fool me. I understood that her appearance was misleading, like mine. There was an air of desperation about her. She looked like she had a razor-thin line, and if you crossed it, you'd wish you hadn't.

I'd watched them at various times, walking through the halls, in the lunchroom, in class. They moved like they existed in a different world than most of us. Like the crowded halls and yelling kids and tired teachers were foreign to them; a flimsy overlay of what truth was playing out in front of their eyes. I understood that, for sure, but my sense was that their world was not only different from the ordinary, mundane one but also different from mine which was occasionally populated by ghosts and monsters.

Travelers. The word floated to the top of my consciousness and bobbed about, not having anything particular to anchor itself to. *Travelers.*

When the bell rang, everyone rocketed out the door. It was a Friday, the sun was shining brightly, and it was one of those first days of spring when the temperature actually got as warm as the bright sunlight promised.

I was occupied trying to cram one more thing into my already loaded backpack when Barb hit me with her knowledge of Charlie's ghost and our dealings with him.

Gulp.

I glanced out the classroom door. Ms. Jackson was occupied, chatting with the teacher across the hall, paying zero attention to us. A million thoughts shot through my brain all at once. *How did they know? What did they know? Who else knew? Was it okay that they knew? Could they see the scary stuff too? Like we could?*

The brilliant reply that actually made it out of my mouth was, "Err . . ."

Man, I'm smooth.

Barb pushed on, brusquely. "We need to walk home with you. Crystal is worried about her sister, and she thinks it may be the kind of weird shit you and your friends mess around with. At least, we're pretty sure nobody else can help."

Crystal said in a near whisper, "Nobody else would believe us."

My heart broke a little for her right then. She looked so sad and so scared. I tried to sound cool and confident, "Sure, yeah. I mean, weird doesn't like, totally scare us off, you know?"

Barb eyeballed me critically, from my messy hair, past my backpack and oboe case to my scuffed up, not-the-fashionable-brand of tennis shoes. I felt I was being judged and found lacking. She glanced dubiously back at Crystal who seemed insistent.

"C'mon," she said shortly. "Let's walk."

Jen had play practice after school, and David had joined the track team, so nobody was waiting for me. I nodded, and we set off.

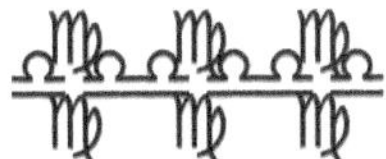

Nobody spoke until we were well off school grounds and away from any of the little groups of kids walking here and there.

"So, go ahead and tell her what happened, Crystal," Barb finally directed, indicating that we were in no danger of being overheard.

Crystal began, her voice low and uncertain as if at any moment someone might yell at her to shut up, or worse.

"It's about Desiree."

"She's your sister?" I asked gently. I had a little bit of experience with super shy people, but I was getting the feeling that Crystal's shyness was more a kind of protective shield than actual insecurity.

"She's my half-sister, but we mostly grew up together. When our mom went to jail, she lucked out and got a great foster family. They have this super nice house in a richy-rich neighborhood, and they're nice people."

I frowned. "You guys couldn't go there together?"

Crystal stopped talking and looked down at the ground.

I cringed. I'd put my foot in it already. "I'm so sorry. I didn't mean to pry . . . please, go on. I'm listening."

She glanced at Barb, as if for permission, and continued carefully. "She'd been there about three months when the weird stuff started happening." She paused again.

"What kind of weird stuff?" I pressed, as gently as I could.

"Like, haunted house stuff, you know? Weird noises, things moving around, lights going on and off, all kinds of crazy shit."

I nodded sagely. In my experience over the last two years, this was pretty tame behavior for a ghost. However, that didn't mean it wasn't a warning of possible escalation. I sensed she wasn't done, so all I said was, "Yeah, I know what you're talking about. What happened next?"

"She ran away. Or at least, that's what everybody is saying." Crystal's chin jutted out and her expression hardened. "She didn't come home from school yesterday."

"You don't believe it?" I asked.

"No way. Totally no way," Crystal replied adamantly. "She freaking loved it there. Her foster mom was super cool. She's a musician and she was teaching Desiree how to play the piano. Even the family's real kids were pretty okay. They'd had a couple of foster kids before that weren't so great, so when Des first got there, it was tough but my little sister is a sweetheart. She's smart and pretty and super funny. She totally made friends with the youngest girl, and they were mega-tight.

"Every time I talked to her on the phone, she just kept on saying how great it was, and how much she wished I could be there too." Crystal's voice wavered a little. "Last weekend, we were making plans to hang out together. I was going to get to spend the night and—"

All these words had tumbled out of Crystal in a rush, and just as suddenly, she seemed to remember where she was and her mouth clamped shut again. She looked around fearfully and took a few fast steps ahead of us.

Barb turned to me, a hot bright anger lit her eyes. "Nobody really gives a shit about kids like us. Foster kids are just a paycheck and an excuse to brag about their charity. If something happens to us, everybody just figures that it was our own fault, anyway."

I frowned, wonderingly. I'd never seen anger like hers before. I didn't understand it. Not then. "Is it any better where you guys are at now? Is it any good being at Whitehall?"

"Ha!" she spit out.

Crystal had stopped a few steps ahead of us and was digging in her second-hand purse. She turned back to me, holding a letter in her hand.

"What's this?" I asked.

"The foster family, the daughter, Beth. She found this letter this morning. She got her brother to drive her over here and drop it off to me before they went to school. That's how I found out Des was gone. It's addressed to 'Sister.' At first, she thought it was for her, but then she read it and got super freaked out."

"Why?" I asked.

"You'll see."

She handed the envelope to me. It looked old fashioned. It was the elegant, small-sized paper that only needs to be folded one time to fit into the little envelopes.

I'd gotten stationery similar to it on Christmas, and it was super pretty, but I never came up with a good enough use for it, so it sat in a box on my desk, looking neat and purposeless. This paper looked old, though. It was heavy, and slightly rough to the touch.

I pulled the letter out and the moment I opened it, a jolt of electricity zipped through me, from my fingertips to my toes. The hairs on the back of my neck jumped to attention. I stood in the warm sunshine and scrubbed at the icy cold goosebumps on my arms.

The handwriting was faded and missing in spots, like a puzzle that was partly obscured. The words that *were* visible looked like they'd been scratched on, with force, as if someone particularly needed those words to be seen. The rest was mostly illegible.

> ~~guy, tricked~~
> ~~basement~~ dark & scary
> in here! ~~blue rock~~
> two other girls ~~one got taken~~
> ~~I'm afraid~~
> ~~house ghost~~
> scared, please
> Cryssybel please help me!

The whole letter had a creepy feel to it, like it wasn't quite . . . of this world. "Is this her handwriting?" I asked.

"No! It isn't. This is all old-fashioned cursive and Des doesn't write like that at all."

I studied the determination on her face. It was obvious that there was no doubt in her mind that this note was from her sister. "Then what makes you know it's for real?" I asked.

She pointed to the last line. "Cryssybel. Nobody else calls me that. Nobody even knows about it. That's Des's special name, just for me." Crystal's face was stricken.

"Angie, I don't know anything about ghosts or weird stuff like that, but I do know about runaways. Nobody cares. Nobody looks very hard for kids like us, not in real life. And if there's some weird dead ghost shit going on . . . I don't," her voice hitched. "Please. Please, you have to help me find my sister."

Barb swung her arm over Crystal's shaking shoulders and turned her slightly away so she could cry without me seeing.

"Can you help her?" she asked me, pointedly. "You and your friends? This is what you do, right?"

"Yeah," I replied, solemnly. "That's what we do. I'll have to talk to my friends. Is there a way you can get us into the foster family's house?"

Barb put a hand on top of Crystal's head and whispered something in her ear. Chrystal scrubbed at her face with her hand and turned to me. "I think so. I'll have to ask Beth . . ." she trailed off.

"Does Beth go to Mickle?" I asked.

"No, they go to the Catholic school over in their neighborhood," she sniffed and straightened her back.

"What about the parents? How much do they know about the ghost stuff?" I asked.

"They don't believe in the ghost. Desiree said they were kind of touchy about it."

"Do you have Beth's phone number on you?" Crystal dug in her purse and produced a folded piece of notebook paper and handed it to me.

"Do you know her last name? Or the address?" I asked, whipping out my pen. She filled in as much detail as she knew.

"Great. I'll get with the others and we'll figure out a plan. If you can, call her and tell her to expect a visit from one of us tonight or in the morning at the latest. We'll figure out some excuse to go over there." I looked at Crystal. The worry and tension were unmistakable in her face. It made me feel bad. Even though my sister wasn't my favorite person in the whole world, if something happened to her — if she went missing like Desiree had — I can't even imagine how scared and worried I'd be. And I'd at least have my mom and dad there to help.

All Crystal had was Barb. And now she had me and Jen and David, too. We would have to be enough.

I really, really hoped we would be enough.

I offered up my strongest, most confident smile. "Try not to worry. We're going to do everything we can to get Desiree home safe."

Crystal mustered a weak smile. Barb nudged her and we separated, me to my house, them down the hill to Whitehall.

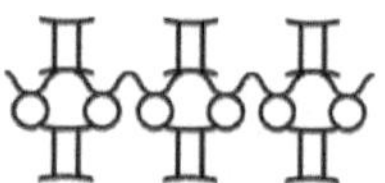

Sprawled out on my bed, iced tea in one hand and pen in the other, I scribbled down some questions I wanted answered from the library before I met with everyone else. I called Mr. Rakow to give him what info I had, and arranged to meet there after supper. Then I pulled what I needed together and jumped on my bike.

Crystal didn't have the house address with her, but she was able to tell me the name of the street and the general area. I needed to get over to the library and have a look at some of the more non-supernatural information sources the library provided, to see if I could gather any history on the neighborhood, or more particularly, about our ghost.

"Hey, Miss Angie. What's new?" asked Jeanne, my favorite Librarian. It was a quiet afternoon, there were only a couple of people in the library besides me.

"Hello, Miss Jeanne!" I responded cheerfully. "I'm doing some research for a project."

"Anything I can help with?"

"I think I have an idea where to start," I replied. I had already flipped through Alan Boye's *Guide to the Ghosts of Lincoln*. I'd been through it several times and didn't recall anything that might fit, but I wanted to rule it out before I started in on the property records and maps.

I was just returning it to its home in the 900's when Jeanne stuck her head around the corner. "Oh dear, is it another of your creepy research topics?"

I tried not to flinch. Jeanne was awesome, but she wasn't officially in the loop. I didn't want to sully her opinion of me or encourage her to mention it to anyone else who might ask a lot of questions, either. But she had helped me out on any number of occasions…

She must have read the dilemma in my expression. For sure, I'm not the best actor of the three of us. Jen took the prize for that, hands down. She glanced back over her shoulder, and satisfied that nobody else needed her help at the moment, came over to where I stood in the stacks.

"Don't worry, Angie. What happens in the library stays here. We're guardians of privacy, don't you know?" She winked. I grinned awkwardly.

"Look," she continued. "I don't know exactly why you need this research, and I don't need to. That's your business. But I'll say this."

I looked at her a little nervously.

"You're a good kid. And I know your dad. I took one of his classes when I was in school."

"You did? You never told me that!"

"It never came up. But the thing is, I can't imagine any child of Professor Parson's doing anything," she paused, searching for the word, "unseemly."

I raised my eyebrows. I flashed back to some moments from my last two years, impaling the demon Mitch with the giant hook at the pool, Mr. Rakow's battle with Charlie's ghost, that thing with the troll under the bridge, and I was suddenly very glad Librarians couldn't read minds.

At least, I hoped they couldn't.

I smiled, doing my best to look like the upstanding child of my upstanding parents. She returned my smile. "If you need help, don't be afraid to ask, okay?"

"Thanks, Miss Jeanne. How far back to you keep the City Directories?" I replied, trying to push away the wiggins her offer of trust had unaccountably given me.

Forty-five minutes later, I glanced at my watch. It wasn't a neat, colorful Swatch like all the popular kids were sporting. Nope. No child of my father's would have anything less than an accurate-to-within-a-fraction-of-a-second Seiko. He'd scammed me into picking ones I liked from a catalog, ostensibly as a Christmas gift for Mom. Instead, he'd splurged and gotten one each for Mom, Mallory and me. No lie, it was awesome and I loved it, but it was yet another nail in the coffin of my aspirations to be even remotely cool.

My tragically unhip timepiece told me that Jen and David would be done soon and I needed to hightail it home.

"I'm out of time for today," I said to Miss Jeanne as I handed back the old City Directories she'd pulled out of Reference for me. "If I need to do some microfilm searching, I'll need to go downtown for that, right?"

"Okay, kiddo. Yes. We have the film for last year's newspapers here, but yes, for anything older than that, you'll have to go to the Main Library, downtown."

"Got it." I loaded my notebooks into my bag. "Is Miss Charlotte still my go-to in the Periodicals Room?"

"Yes, Charlotte or Miss Kim, depending on the day. Feel free to call ahead if you have exact dates, they can have things out and ready for you."

"Awesome! Thank you so much!" I shouldered my backpack and headed for the door.

⁂

I was too out of breath from standing on the pedals to get up the hill to holler at Jen and David when I spotted them up ahead. I caught up with them about a block from my house, and filled them in between gulps of air.

"So, what's the plan, Ang?" David asked.

"I think getting inside the house is going to be our best bet. If we can connect with the ghost, we might be able to figure out exactly what's going on. Crystal is sure the ghost had something to do with Desiree's disappearance, but something about that just doesn't feel right to me. Your mom or Mr. Rakow might have some thoughts about who it might be, and I want to know if they've ever even heard of ghosts spiriting people away."

"Ha ha, punny," David chuckled.

"Or if something totally different is going on," I continued, rolling my eyes.

We arrived at my house, just in time to see my mom pull in the driveway.

"Meet you guys at Mr. Rakow's after supper?"

"Yeah, just call when you're done," Jen said. "I may have an idea for getting us into the house, I think one of Beth's older brothers is on the debate team at the Catholic High School."

"Cool," I replied, relieved. I was sure whatever Jen was cooking up would be clever and surprising. It always was. "See you guys later."

I rushed inside to knock out my math homework before I had to set the table.

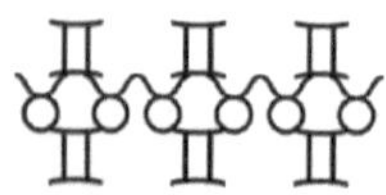

Dinner that night was leftovers — the last of the ham and scalloped potatoes from Sunday, plus a little vegetable soup from Wednesday. Mallory dumped a bag of frozen corn into a pan on the stove and stirred in the butter and salt while I ran to the basement refrigerator to retrieve the last few slices of mom's cherry jello salad dessert. It had cream cheese frosting and was kind of addictive. Dad was putting ice in the water glasses on the table when I came back up.

"Hey kiddo. How was school?"

"Okay, we have end of quarter tests next week, and then I think we get Friday off."

"We have Thursday *and* Friday off next week," interjected Mallory. Trust my sister to have memorized all our days off from school.

"Great!" Mom chimed in. "Both of you girls need to do a deep clean on your rooms. Don't make any plans for your days off until that's done. Sheets and dirty laundry down the laundry chute, rugs vacuumed, books and records organized and clean clothes put away, please."

"Gawd, Mom!" Mallory groaned. Our mom ignored her with the ease of long practice.

I was too busy thinking about Desiree to raise much fuss. It wasn't a huge deal, anyway. It's not like our rooms were that big or anything. It was maybe a half hour of work, but Mallory always acted like it was the end of the world.

We sat and Dad gave our standard supper blessing. My folks were regular church goers, but they didn't always go to the same church. Mal and I had always gone along. Dad was big on us knowing stuff about lots of different religious traditions. He and mom both encouraged us to learn and experiment before we ever settled on how we wanted to make church a part of our own adult lives. It was an unusual way to be raised, but I think it served both of us well.

"You look particularly pensive this evening, Angie. Is it anything suitable for dinner table conversation?" my Dad asked.

"I'm not sure," I mused, trying to force my thoughts into something sharable. "I talked to some girls at school today, who live over at Whitehall."

"What the heck were you talking to those kids for, Ang?" my sister said in a superior tone. "They're trouble. You should stay away."

"When did *you* become my moral compass?" I shot back. "Like, was it before or after you dated that kid Kevin, who ended up getting kicked out of school and sent to juvie?"

"That's my point, exactly *Angel*," she sneered. "You're too little and innocent to know who *is* trouble and who isn't. I have *experience*."

"Okay, you two," Dad interrupted. "Angie, please continue."

"We were talking about a girl they know who ran away. Or at least that's the story, but nobody knows for sure, and that made this girl, Barb, super mad. She said nobody cares about kids like them. She said, if one of them disappears, folks just shrug and say, *another runaway*. Like they don't look for them or care if something really happened to them or anything.

"Is that true? I mean, if Mallory or I disappeared, you guys would go crazy with the police, and newspapers and milk cartons and the whole nine yards, wouldn't you?"

My mom, who had paled visibly at the mention of something happening to me or my sister, responded. "We most certainly would!"

"So, what's the deal with these kids? I mean, is it just because they don't have parents like you who would freak out and alert the presses? Is it the places they live, like Whitehall, just don't make a big public stink? Or is it the kids?" I continued. "Did they like, give up their shot at being loved and missed when they went into foster care or got in trouble?"

The table had gotten quiet.

"Like, not all of those kids did something bad, you

know, Mal? Crystal, Barb's friend, she's in Whitehall because her mom went to jail and she didn't have anybody else to take care of her. She's never done anything wrong, but if she disappeared, would anybody even care?"

Dad spoke, thoughtfully. "I know what you mean, Angie. Of course, the folks who work at Whitehall would notify the police immediately if one of their kids disappeared, and I'm sure that some of them would take a personal interest, but I don't know how far they'd be able to take it.

"I worked with the Board at Whitehall last year on that project for the new Social Sciences building on campus. They're good folks, caring and responsible people who want to make things better in our community, but they have their hands very full. Did you know there's a waiting list to even get into Whitehall? There aren't enough beds to go around to take care of all the kids who need places to stay.

"And Angie is right, Mallory. The kids who have committed any kind of more serious offenses are not housed there, but in other facilities. Whitehall is sort of a middle step for kids who are in between tough family situations, foster care, and the police. It's a tricky place for those kids to be, and the staff is overwhelmed by their numbers. They do the best they can, but it's true. Sometimes kids fall through the cracks." He frowned and shook his head, picking at the ham on his plate.

"I bet, too," my mom mused, "particularly with runaways, it's got to be incredibly difficult for the staff there to take their attention away from the needs of the kids they have right in front of them and try to focus on the kids who aren't there. Someone else has to take over, I guess. The police, or . . ." she trailed off.

I knew the answer to that, or at least my part of it.

Something Lost

For Desiree, if nobody else had time to care, then it became our job.

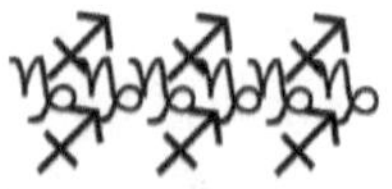

After we'd cleared up the supper dishes, I went to my room to gather my notes and things to go to Mr. Rakow's. I pulled Phyllida's magic book from its hiding place at the bottom of my desk drawer. I had started out with it under my mattress, but the dang thing gave me super weird dreams, so I moved it. I flopped down on my bed and flipped through the pages.

"Okay, Phyllida, what do you have to tell me? We have ghosts and either runaways or kidnappers, but we don't know which. Or maybe it's something else. Maybe it was an accident or Desiree is lost or sick someplace. Can you help me find a lost girl?"

I paused when my fingers tingled and lay the book open flat. Letters formed of shiny purple ink began to appear in the margins of the page.

> *Lost is a vast country, child. Many reside therein. Some wander the folds and planes of the landscape, seeking ease from suffering. Others seek only escape back to the real world. A chosen few travel there for higher purpose.*

"How do we find Desiree?" I murmured quietly to the book. "Is she trying to come back home?"

> *Beware the grayness; it is far more dangerous than it appears. The girl has one foot in the country of Lost, and one foot firmly planted here, but not for long. She needs her*

defender to anchor her. Time is short, scholar. Before the sun falls tomorrow, the child will be beyond your help. Use the enchantment on this page to open your eyes so you may see past the grayness. Do not fail. This girl holds the key.

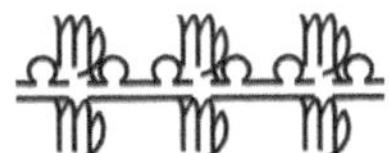

I got to Mr. Rakow's house first. He had already pulled the extra chairs up to the kitchen table and set out iced tea.

"Did you figure out the exact house number where Beth lives, Angie?" Mr. Rakow asked, pulling out a map of Lincoln.

"Yes, I found them in the City Directory by name," I responded. "It's here, on Piedmont Street." I handed him a sheet of paper with my notes from earlier, along with the cryptic note from Crystal.

Mr. Rakow frowned and peered at the map. Shadow got up from his spot under the kitchen table next to Mr. Rakow's feet and moved to sit expectantly at the door. I followed, knowing David and Jen must be coming up the walk.

I opened the door, and David, Jen and Lorraine piled in, still laughing at something David had said. "Hey guys!" I greeted them, bumping Shadow lightly with my leg to make room in the doorway. He obliged and nuzzled my hand with his nose as I pushed the door shut behind us. We all clambered in around the kitchen table. Shadow resumed his spot by Mr. Rakow's feet.

"Did you guys figure out who our ghost is this time?" David asked. "Jen can get inside tomorrow afternoon."

"How'd you manage that so quickly?" I asked, impressed.

"Beth's brother Matt is on the Pius High School debate team. Alan, you know Alan, the tall kid from drama club? He's kind of interested in joining debate, plus he knows the family from his old church, so he called, and we're set to go over at 1:00 so Matt can give him the lowdown. Crystal called ahead to let Beth know we were coming. So, while the guys chat, Beth is going to show me around the house where they've seen their ghost." Jen peered intently at an invisible chip on one of her very long fingernails while she gave her report.

I nodded. Jen knew somebody everywhere. It never took long, anytime she went someplace new, within minutes she had a crowd looking to her, and she invariably walked away with a notebook page full of names and phone numbers.

I squashed down a tickle of jealousy. I was never a hundred percent sure if I felt that particular jealousy because it was so easy for her to make friends, or if it was pure selfishness on my part. Either way, I knew it was uncalled for, and I did my best to remind myself that if I wanted to make more friends, I wasn't totally incapable, and also that Jen loved me and we were solid.

It mostly worked.

I took a breath, nudged my better self, and said sincerely, "Awesome, you're the best, Jen."

"So, Lorraine, does this address that Miss Angie found ring any bells with you?" Mr. Rakow asked passing her my sheet of notes, his lips drawn into a frown.

"Oof. It's the O'Shea house, isn't it?" Lorraine asked.

"Yep."

"What's the O'Shea house?" David, Jen and I all

asked in one breath.

"Almost twenty years ago, the lady of the house, Mary O'Shea, was murdered there, by a man who was doing some work for a neighbor." Mr. Rakow frowned.

"What is it?" I asked. We'd spent enough time together that I was well schooled in most of his expressions. This one meant there was something he was reluctant to share.

Lorraine spoke up. "It was bad, as I recall. The older kids were still at school when it happened, but one or two of her youngest were at home."

I blanched. Some of the stuff we dealt with gave *me* nightmares, and it was only knowing I wasn't alone in this that made some of it bearable. *Little kids? Preschool age? Wow.* Not for the first time did I secretly hope there was a special Hell reserved for the monsters who did such things.

"So, wait, who are we dealing with? Is it Mrs. O'Shea's ghost? Or is it the killer? Or, please don't tell me something happened to one of the little kids," Jen said, her voice turning growly.

"Let me see the note," said Lorraine. Mr. Rakow handed it over.

She looked it over. "Trick . . . locked in . . . basement . . . blue rock . . . other girls. What other girls? Have there been any other reports of missing children?"

I recalled our conversation from dinner earlier, and my stomach clenched.

Mr. Rakow got up from the kitchen table and went to the doughboy where he kept his newspapers. I have no idea why those hinged tables on either side of the sofa were named after either baker's journeymen or WWI foot soldiers. That's a linguistic mystery I have yet to unravel. While he flipped through for news articles on missing kids, Lorraine continued to frown at the note in her hand.

"What is it, mom?" Jen asked. "Are you getting a vibe?"

"I am. There's definitely an energy residue of some kind here. Do you want to give it a try?"

"Sure. Mr. Rakow, do you mind if I use the recliner?" Her eyes twinkled but I still didn't find the whole thing terribly funny. A few months ago, we'd discovered that sometimes Jen's prophecies could be triggered by handling an object that had been in contact with a supernatural creature or event.

We'd been trying to suss out the identity of a beastie who was haunting the underside of a bridge over Salt Creek. Jen had picked up a tennis shoe Mr. Rakow had found in the vicinity, and it had given her a full body prophecy. She was sitting on one of the hard chairs around Mr. Rakow's kitchen table at the time and had been tossed from her seat to the floor. She'd bashed her head on the corner of the stove on the way down.

A trip to the Emergency Room and six stitches later, we changed our methods on how to hand Jen potentially prophecy-laden objects.

She and Lorraine went into the living room, and Jen made herself comfy on Mr. Rakow's big old worn recliner. I followed and pulled the side table with the lamp a few more inches away for good measure.

Lorraine held the letter out, and Jen took it carefully. She closed her eyes, her long thin fingers trailing over the thick stationery. For a minute, I didn't think anything was going to happen but then Jen's back straightened and her expression changed. Telltale signs that she was on the receiving end of some kind of message from — well, from *wherever* her messages came.

"Speak, baby," said Lorraine softly. "What do you

see?"

"Mother. Sweet mother . . . kids laughing. White gloves and pearls. Kisses . . . sugar cookies."

Jen had drawn herself up in the chair primly and folded her hands. I swear, I could almost smell sugar cookies baking. Then her expression shifted to one of worried alarm.

"The children! No! Don't take the children!" Jen jumped up out of the chair, her hands outstretched and shaking. "Not the children!"

Lorraine and I stood close by, ready to swoop in and catch her if she fell or anything, but we didn't touch her. Lorraine said the prophecies were a bit like sleepwalking, and touching her during one might interrupt the flow, so we tried to keep our hands off as long as she wasn't hurting herself.

Jen slumped back down in the chair, still agitated and muttering, "He's not your friend. Stay away! Must protect the children!" Then she was still. A moment later she straightened up and scrubbed at her face like she was coming out of a deep sleep.

"Children? Her children?" Mr. Rakow asked from the kitchen doorway.

David came in carrying Jen's iced tea that he'd topped up to the brim. She took it gratefully and chugged half. Apparently, prophecies were a thirsty business.

"I'm not sure, exactly," Jen hesitated.

"How could it be her children if Jen's seeing the future?" I asked.

"Are ghost timelines the same as ours?" David wondered.

"And what does it mean when a ghost wants to *protect* someone?" Mr. Rakow asked pointedly.

Lorraine was kneeling beside Jen, one hand stroking

her hair. "Good question," she said thoughtfully. "I can't think of any ghosts I've ever heard of who retained much logic or good decision-making prowess after their demise."

"What about Pansy?" I asked.

"Good point," Lorraine conceded. Pansy was Caril's grandmother, the one who had helped us put Charlie back in his box after that bizarre tornado had let him out and deposited him and his creepy car at our school.

"Is there a chance that our ghosty kidnapped Desiree to keep her safe from something?" I interjected.

"Maybe," Mr. Rakow said. "Or maybe to keep her safe from something she *thinks* is a danger."

"Oh jeez," I sighed. "So, we might have a ghost kidnapping kids because she's got issues, or we might have a ghost kidnapping kids to keep them safe from something even worse?"

"Or we could be totally off base, and it's something none of us has figured out yet," sighed Lorraine.

"Getting inside the house should help," mused Jen.

"I'm coming with you," Lorraine said decidedly. "Even if Beth's mom isn't home, I'll come up with some reason to go in with you guys. I believe I have a way we can thin the veil slightly in the house, make it easier for us to connect with whatever spirits are residing there. I'll put the spell ingredients together tonight."

"David, Angie, I want you two with me," said Mr. Rakow, categorically.

"Are we doing recon?" David asked, his face alight.

"You got it, kid. We'll scout the area for clues while Jen and Lorraine are inside. Come on, let's take a look at this map and decide on our strategy."

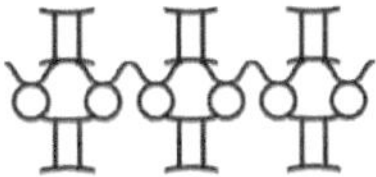

We took two cars on Saturday. Jen and Alan went with Lorraine to go inside the house. Alan's family used to go to the same church as Beth's, so there was plenty of legitimate connection there to get Lorraine and Jen inside.

I hurried up just as Jen and Lorraine took off. It had taken me more time to execute the enchantment from Phyllida's book than I'd thought. I was careful to get the water blessed and infused and magicked up and splashed in my eyes just like the book said. I was a little worried it would sting, but it hadn't. I hadn't seen anything out of the ordinary on the way over, but Phyllida's spells had proven helpful in the past, so I was confident this one would work, as long as I had done all the steps correctly.

There were two surprises for me when I climbed into Mr. Rakow's Nova. The first was Jon. He and David were dressed in running shorts and tennies. At Lorraine's urging, Jon had gone running a few times with David, enough to realize he really disliked it, I guess. They'd developed a compromise where Jon would ride along with David on his bike to keep him company, which in turn kept Lorraine from worrying about David being out running on his own for long periods of time. She was forever concerned he would twist an ankle and have to limp five miles home. I assumed Jon's bike was in the trunk. Between the two boys in the back seat sat Shadow.

The second surprise was completely awesome. The passenger seat was occupied by a gorgeous, leggy German Shepherd pup.

"Who is this sweet bundle of awesome?" I bubbled as Mr. Rakow held the gangly pup back so I could climb in.

"This is Alesta," he replied. "It's sort of an emergency foster situation. There's a German Shepherd rescue place coming to get her, but they can't take her until middle of next week, so she's staying with us for a few days."

I slid into the passenger seat, fastened my seat belt and held my arms out. Mr. Rakow directed Alesta back in the direction of my lap. She was young and awkward, but I could feel the power and vitality of her. When she was grown, she was going to be every bit as ferocious and badass as Shadow. "How old is she?"

"Close to six months, but she's smaller than she should be. She's been living on the streets; looks like food has been pretty scarce."

"Hey sweet girl," I mumbled into her fur. Alesta was far more interested in looking out the window than listening to compliments, but she gave me a polite nose lick and allowed me to rub behind her ears most of the way across town.

Pure bliss.

When we drove past Whitehall, I noticed some kids outside playing basketball. I wondered if Barb and Crystal were there, but the courts were too far away for me to tell from the street. *Wish us luck,* I thought as we sped by.

Mr. Rakow pulled the car into a lot adjacent to a neighborhood park and popped the trunk. While Jon retrieved his bike, Mr. Rakow and I sorted out dogs and leashes, and David stretched and jogged in place.

Mr. Rakow turned to the boys. "You two take the north half of the neighborhood like we planned. Run the grid, keep your eyes open, and work your way south, toward the house. We'll take the south side. Pay special attention to anything with a line of sight to the house, but don't rule out other options. This is recon. We're looking for anything that seems out of the ordinary for Mr. and Mrs. Upper Middle-Class Homeowner. Overgrown brush concealing a property. A vehicle with few or obscured windows. Excessive security. Anything resembling the 'blue rock' mentioned in the note. Of course, any signs of a struggle or anything chaotic or anyone who raises your hackles. Use your instincts. Plan to be near the house in thirty minutes. Jon, is your walkie on?"

Jon reached out to the walkie talkie he and David had affixed to the handlebars of his bike. He flipped it on and clicked the transmit button a few times so we could hear the resulting clicks on Mr. Rakow's end.

"Excellent. Lorraine and Jenny have one with them, make sure yours stays on, and you're paying attention. Eyes sharp, watch your backs. See you in thirty."

The boys nodded sharply and took off to the north. Mr. Rakow and I headed east toward our corner of the grid. The boys had a larger space to cover, but Beth's house was in our portion of the search area. We crossed the one busy street that ran diagonally through the neighborhood and began our mission.

I had to keep reminding myself to pay attention to the search, and not Alesta's beautiful shining fur or adorable leggy gait. I'd always wanted a pet, but my mom's and Mallory's allergies were dreadful, so it was out of the question until I was out on my own. I'd daydreamed about a zillion times about getting a puppy and a kitten at the same time so they could grow up together.

I gave myself a mental thwack and scanned the area we were passing through for anything hinky. Mr. Rakow instructed me to stay either behind or beside him and Shadow. He wanted to give Alesta the benefit of watching Shadow's good behavior. Good behavior would make her more appealing to a new family, which was the next step to finding her a forever home.

"She hasn't had any experience leash walking, Angie. Don't let her pull, or stop and sniff for too long. Keep her walking."

"She's doing great so far, Mr. Rakow," I responded besottedly.

"That's great, keep one eye on her, and one on our job."

"Yes, Sar'nt," I replied, that particular pronunciation of *Sergeant* was a subtle nuance I'd picked up listening to Mr. Rakow's Army stories.

He rolled his eyes, a not so subtle nuance he'd picked up from watching me. About a block up ahead I spotted a lady walking her Boxer.

"Do we stop?" I asked.

"Nope. Walk behind us, Angie. Keep her walking, right by your feet, eyes on Shadow like nothing is different. We want them to pass each other calmly. Think *calm*."

I dropped behind him and kept Alesta close to me on my right, so I was between her and the approaching pair, mimicking Mr. Rakow and Shadow. Probably my absolute confidence in Mr. Rakow and Shadow was the biggest help I could give Alesta, but even so, I saw the look of concern in the approaching woman's eyes, and I knew that *she* wasn't feeling the calm.

Sure enough, she pulled her Boxer off the sidewalk and almost into the street to go around us while her Boxer danced and lunged wildly. Shadow, of course, was completely unflappable. He had eyes for Mr. Rakow alone. Alesta spared the barker a look, but instead of cringing away, or lunging forward, she maneuvered her little puppy self in between the Boxer and me, like she was protecting me, and continued walking sedately forward.

"Is that usual puppy behavior?" I asked Mr. Rakow once we were past the pair.

Mr. Rakow, who had turned in time to observe her move, was staring with eyebrows raised. "Nope." He shook his head like he knew more than he was letting on, but wasn't sure he believed it.

We continued on, Mr. Rakow and Shadow alert, me beaming with wonderment at Alesta, and trying my hardest to be on the lookout for anything blue or spooky or out of place.

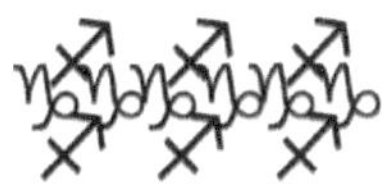

Barb watched a Chevy Nova drive past on the main street in front of the mansion, headed west and felt an unexplainable pull. She glanced around at the crowd of kids who'd been let outside to work off some steam. Crystal was sitting by herself in the grass, chewing her fingernails and twisting her hair. She was a nervous wreck, and it was grating on Barb.

Barb had never been good at waiting around. She'd always been better at moving. She'd felt for a while now that her time at this place was coming to an end, and now she was sure of it. She felt for the kitchen knife she'd snagged last night and made sure it was still secure in the hidden jeans pocket she'd fashioned for herself. The only good thing about that fricking Home-Ec class.

Some kids had gathered at the other end of the basketball court, a sure sign of trouble. Barb spotted Jose in the middle of the pack, showing off his latest piece of contraband. That did it. Her decision was made.

"Crystal, let's go." Crystal didn't ask any questions, just jumped up and followed. Barb led the way right into the middle of the group of boys.

She elbowed a couple of them out of the way so she could see Jose. He'd been in and out of trouble since he arrived and was forever getting busted with one thing or another. "What's that?" She demanded, pointing.

"Wouldn't you like to know?" He crowed, looking around for the other boys to back him up — nobody bit. Jose may have been around for a while, but so had Barb, and most of these boys knew what she was capable of, a couple of them knew it up close and personal. Jose was good at getting hold of things, but he wasn't very smart.

Barb shoved him against the metal pole to which the basketball hoop was affixed and asked again, politely, her forearm on his throat. "What is it?"

"Jeez girl, can't you take a joke? It's a wrist rocket."

Barb grabbed his arm and examined it. It had a brace that wrapped around the forearm, with an attached handle that you gripped with your fist. On top were two big industrial sized rubber bands with a pocket in the center. Essentially a souped-up slingshot. It looked dangerous as hell.

"Where'd you get it?"

"Lifted it."

"What ammo do you use?"

"Rocks work unless you have these." With his free hand, he reached in his pocket and drew out a palm full of metal ball bearings. Barb smiled.

"You're going to give those to me."

"You're gonna have to make me!" Jose retorted, but there was fear in his eyes.

He was right to be afraid.

Five minutes later, Crystal, Barb and the wrist rocket,

along with a pocket full of ball bearings were sneaking off campus and heading toward Beth's house.

"How are we going to get all the way across town, Barb?" Crystal asked. "I'm not even sure of the way."

"I am. I looked at the map in the phone book last night when Miss Clark was taking care of Michelle after Lisa ripped her fingernail off."

"That was gross."

"Yeah, but she was asking for it. Anyway, I figured out the route. If we can't hitch a ride, we'll just walk. C'mon."

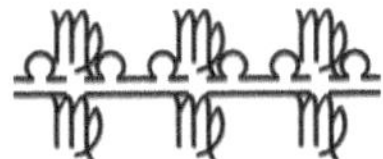

Mr. Rakow and I executed our grid pattern of the neighborhood for the next twenty minutes, making our way on our preordained path toward Beth's house. On our way, we fielded more than one admiring glance from neighborhood dog lovers. They were just as captivated as I was by the sight of little Alesta, trotting along with Shadow like she was just the smartest and best pup in the whole world. I was head over heels in love with her already, entertaining secret thoughts of housing her at Mr. Rakow's until I was old enough to move out amid other hopeless daydreams.

When a couple of elementary school-aged kids scrambled up to us and asked if they could pet her, Mr. Rakow gave his blessing. He also wordlessly indicated to me that I should do my part and pump the neighborhood children for information about our missing girl. Fortunately, one of them was wearing a t-shirt with the school logo on it, so I didn't have to fish around to see if they went to the same school as Beth and Desiree.

"You guys go to St. Teresa's?" I asked the older of the two, a girl who looked to be about nine or ten.

"Yeah," she responded distractedly, her eyes locked on Alesta who was playing her part as if she'd trained for it; being adorable, licking hands and letting the girl and her little brother pet her without hesitation. "I'm in fourth grade."

"Oh yeah? Do you know my friend Beth? She's a sixth grader there."

The girl pondered this information with all the careful attentiveness one might expect from a fourth grader petting a puppy, and shook her head.

"Or the girl who stays with her, Desiree?"

The girl didn't respond, but her little brother cocked an eyebrow and peered up at me from under his mop of dark, curly hair.

"Desiree is the girl that got lost, right? 'Member, Becca? Mom was telling Daddy about it last night at supper."

Becca took advantage of her brother's distraction to take over petting Alesta's tummy.

"Oh no! She got lost? What happened?" I asked, trying to sound impressed that he knew some juicy gossip.

"Dunno. Mom told Daddy that she was playing with some bad boys and she probably ran off with them, but the ladies from the church were all upset about it."

"Bad boys? That sounds dangerous. You wouldn't ever mess around with bad kids, would you?"

"Oh no," he shook his head solemnly. "Mama says to stay away from the white house with the motorcycles. She says the boy who lives there and his friends are all troublemakers, and we shouldn't talk to them, so we don't go down the busy street, not ever." He gestured vaguely toward Cotner Blvd, the busy street that bisected the neighborhood.

"That's good; you should totally listen to your mom. Moms are the best at keeping us safe. Speaking of which, is that yours waving to you?" I asked.

The kids turned and spotted their mom at the front door of a brick house, two doors down. Becca took off immediately, hollering, "Come on, Mikey!"

Mikey paused and straightened up. In a practiced and very polite tone, he said "Thank you for letting us pet your dogs. They are very good dogs!"

"You're welcome, kid. You keep on being a good boy and do what your mom says, okay?" responded Mr. Rakow.

"Yes sir!" and he was off, scampering up to his porch to be greeted with an embrace and a kiss on the head. I sighed. I wished everybody could have a mom like that, or like mine or Jen's. It just seemed to make the world spin more happily.

"That's Beth's house, just there," Mr. Rakow said, indicating with a nod of his head. I say we walk past it, and around the corner. I'd like to see the house with the motorcycles, where the troublemakers live."

"Yes, sir!" I replied, giving Alesta and Shadow each a rub on the head.

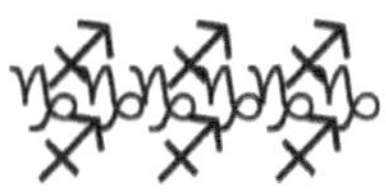

I glanced at Lorraine's parked car as we passed, wondering what was going on inside the house. It was a low, dark red brick house with lots of pretty flowers and bushes planted artistically around the front door and walkway. It looked like a happy place, not a spooky, haunted one but of course, I didn't get any details until afterward, when Jen and Lorraine and everyone else gave me their full accounts, all of which I, of course, dutifully transcribed.

According to them, when they first arrived, Lorraine accompanied Jenny and Alan to the front door. Beth's mom answered and welcomed Alan like an old friend, even though it had been over a year since his family had moved to a different neighborhood and changed parishes.

Alan introduced her to Jen and Lorraine, and Beth's mom took Lorraine into the kitchen for coffee while the kids took over the living room. The boys were immediately engaged in an in-depth conversation about the intricacies of debate; who were the best coaches, the best school's teams, and the toughest individual competitors.

Jen and Beth took their opportunity to skedaddle as quickly as they could and headed for Desiree's room, which was on the opposite side of the house from the kitchen.

"This is where I found the letter, right here!" exclaimed Beth, breathlessly, pointing at the desk.

"Did you show it to your mom or dad before you took it to Crystal?" Jen asked.

"No! No way. Mom and Dad both are totally freaked out by ghosts. They say they don't believe our ghost is real, but I think they just say that because that's what they want us to believe. For the longest time, they tried to keep us from finding out we live in a murder house, but of course, all my brothers' friends knew about it and talked about all the time. Mom and Dad were super upset when they found out we all knew."

"Were you? Freaked out, I mean," Jen asked, looking around the bedroom.

"No, not really," Beth replied, thoughtfully. "For real, it was kind of a relief. I mean, I knew since before I was even in kindergarten that weird stuff happened in our house."

"Like what?" Jen asked.

"Like, the floor in one corner of the living room is always super cold. Mom tried to put our real Christmas tree in that corner one year, and all the needles dried up and fell off the first night. They said it must have been a sick tree and took it out. They bought the artificial tree that year, and that's what we've had ever since."

"Wow!" said Jen, encouragingly. Clearly, this was a topic Beth liked, and she was relishing being able to share with an appreciative audience. As she continued to speak, Jen canvassed the room, brushing surfaces lightly with her fingertips, searching for any signs of ghostly activity.

"Yeah! Sometimes the lights in this room turn on and off, that's how Desiree figured it out. But the ghosty lady didn't scare her either."

"No?" Jen asked, reaching for the light switch. It had one of those decorative switch-plate covers on it. This one looked like an angel from some renaissance painting. She didn't touch it, the vibe coming off of it was strong enough for Jen to feel from a foot away.

"Nah. I mean, the ghost isn't really scary at all. In fact, it's more like the opposite," Beth mused.

"Oh yeah, like how?" Jen asked.

"She likes us. She saved us all one time, right after New Year's when I was in third grade."

"She saved you?" Jen asked, eyes wide.

"Totally. It was the middle of the night, and all the smoke alarms started beeping and woke us all up. We couldn't smell any fire, but Mom and Dad ran us all over to the neighbor's house anyway and called the Fire

Department. When the fire-fighters got inside, they heard banging down in the basement, so they went downstairs. They came running back out of the house saying something was wrong with our furnace They said it was leaking a super dangerous gas, and that if we hadn't all gotten out of the house, we could have *died*."

"Oh, wow! Really?"

"Totally. But the weird part was, they couldn't figure out why our smoke alarms had gone off because that gas doesn't make any smoke. Plus, the one right by the basement door didn't even have a battery in it. Dad had checked them all before Christmas, and he was going to replace that one because it didn't work right, but he hadn't yet. And it was going off anyway."

"That's amazing. And you're for sure it was the ghost?"

"For sure," Beth replied in all seriousness.

"Has she ever tried to talk to you?" Jen asked.

"No, not really. Sometimes I see her, though. Mostly she smiles at me, kind of a sad smile. And one time when Mom and Dad were out late at a party and our dumb babysitter, Tiffany, didn't care that I had a bad dream, she came and sat and rocked in the rocking chair that used to be in my room and I heard music."

"Music? Like, she was singing?"

"No, it was an instrument. Like what angels play."

"A harp?"

"Yeah. It was really nice. She sat and rocked, and the music played. I wasn't scared at all."

"She's never acted scary at all, huh?"

"Never. She's a good ghost. Maybe even an angel. That's what Mom would say, probably."

"You know what? I've seen one other ghost who did the same thing, tried to help people. Maybe she was an angel too. I think you're lucky to have her here."

"Me too! And that's why I think she's trying to help Desiree. I don't believe Des ran away, but I don't know how to find her. I don't know what the ghosty lady is trying to tell me, and I really want Des back." Tears welled in Beth's eyes when she said that.

Jen put an arm around the girl and squeezed her shoulders. She glanced up as a faint glowing pulsed through the walls of the room and then faded. She smiled. "I have an idea that might help us find her. Do you still have that rocking chair? The one that used to be in your room?"

Beth's face brightened. "Yeah! It's in mom's sewing room! I'll show you!"

The sewing room was at the back of the house, facing the back yard. It was a little room, too small to be a proper bedroom, but a good fit for a sewing machine, a scuffed up wooden table that might have once seated four in an old-fashioned kitchen, and a few shelves full of fabrics, threads, and patterns. The rocking chair sat in front of the room's only window.

Jen looked at the chair and looked at Beth. The girl's eyes were bright with worry, and a fierce desire to help her foster sister.

"Do you feel brave?" Jen asked, a lilting challenge in her voice.

Beth grinned brazenly.

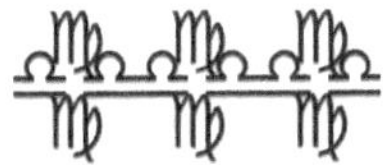

Mr. Rakow and I walked the dogs down to the corner past Beth's house and hung a right. The sidewalk along Cotner was narrower than on the side streets, and the houses were a little smaller. They were still nice, but not quite as nice as Beth's house. The smallest of these sat about halfway down the block, and its driveway sported not only a Harley Davidson, but also a sports car under a tarp, and a couple of dirt bikes leaning up against the garage. The garage door was open, and two lawn chairs were placed near the opening, with an upturned hubcap in between, overflowing with cigarette butts and ashes.

This had to be the place.

Since there wasn't quite enough room for us to walk side by side here, Mr. Rakow and Shadow had dropped behind Alesta and me. Alesta thought being in front was a fine idea, and she trotted along next to me like she was Queen of all she surveyed.

As we approached, a tall, thin guy with wavy brown hair and deep-set brown eyes stepped out of the garage and sauntered over to the Harley. He unfolded a little camp stool, perched on it and opened the tool kit he'd carried in his other hand, all without dropping the ash off the cigarette he held between his lips. He was B-movie star good looking, almost like Chachi Arcola from *Happy Days*, and clearly, he knew it. One could almost hear the director calling, "Action!" in this dude's movie version of his own life.

I heard Mr. Rakow give a quietly derisive snort. I had to agree. Despite the initial flutter I'd felt when his brown eyes casually passed over me, his whole display was pretty scripted. I walked on, trying to anticipate how this was going to play out.

"Nice looking dogs," he drawled as I walked by, but his eyes weren't on the dogs. I fought to keep from rolling my eyes. Honestly, guys could be so gross. He had to be at least twenty-one, almost ten years older than me. And Mr. Rakow was *right there*. Ugh.

I dropped my cloak of stupidity over my IQ, giggled and said, "Thanks!"

Mr. Rakow and Shadow stepped up next to me on the sidewalk, and suddenly Hotstuff had both eyes on his bike.

"Hey," he nodded toward Mr. Rakow.

Mr. Rakow grunted something indecipherable and put a hand on my shoulder. "C'mon kiddo. I think the dogs are getting hungry. You know how this big guy gets when he's hungry." He made a nearly imperceptible hand motion and Shadow, who was directly in front our Chachi Arcola's perch at that second, let out a low, deep, rumbling almost-growl. It even made the hair stand up on the back of *my* neck.

I heard, rather than saw the screech of the folding stool's metal legs as our friend leapt awkwardly back away from Shadow, who sauntered slowly on by, next to Mr. Rakow.

Alesta hadn't strayed more than two inches from my legs this whole time, and I noticed just then that her hackles were raised. Her eyes were on Shadow, and I really believe that if he'd made a move for the dude, Alesta would have raced in, teeth bared. They were both giving me the impression that they really would have enjoyed a bite of jerk.

Once we got out of earshot, I asked Mr. Rakow, "What do you make of him?"

"He's a predator. I could smell it on him. I wouldn't be surprised at all if he had a hand in this mess. He looks right for the part."

"What part, though?

"I'm not sure yet, but I feel like we're getting warm.

Keep your eyes peeled, Angie."

Just then, Mr. Rakow's walkie-talkie crackled. He pulled it off his belt and listened carefully.

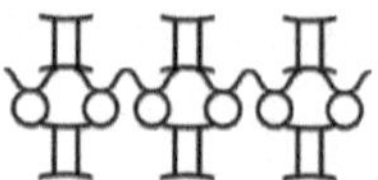

Beth's mom, Shannon, led Lorraine through the house to the kitchen, where she settled her in a sunny nook and produced coffee and a warm cinnamon cake with crumble topping.

"This is outstanding. Did you make it this morning?" Lorraine asked through a mouthful.

"No, my neighbor, Janet did. She brought it over with that basket of fruit," Shannon said, distractedly rinsing out a dishcloth.

Lorraine looked around the kitchen noting, for the first time, what seemed to be an awful lot of covered dishes. She paused, cake halfway to her mouth and said, "I'm so terribly sorry. We've come at a really awful time for you, haven't we? Alan's folks, Jack and Cheryl, they mentioned something about a foster daughter of yours who'd run away."

Shannon's mouth drew down with worry. She paced from one end of the kitchen counter to the other, scrubbing at invisible specs on its immaculate surface. "Yes, I mean, we think so. That's what the police said, anyway, that we shouldn't panic and she'll probably turn up, but foster kids do run away pretty often, I guess."

She took a deep, shuddery breath and ran her cloth under steaming hot water from the tap. "I don't know, though. I mean, Desiree never seemed as distant as some of the other kids we've fostered, I thought she was adjusting well. I really didn't expect anything like this to happen. I'm just so worried! My husband took our three youngest over to their grandparents' house for the day, and he's gone to speak to an attorney. There has to be something we can do. Beth and I wanted to stay here, you know, in case Desiree came home."

"Oh, you poor dear, here you are taking care of me when you're the one who needs some taking care of. Come and sit right down. That counter is clean enough, and your poor hands are just red from the hot water. Come on now, for a moment and just breathe!"

Lorraine jumped up and led Shannon by the shoulders over to a seat near the sunny window. She took the cloth from her hands poured her a fresh cup of coffee. "Do you take cream, hon?" she asked, reaching for the refrigerator.

"Oh yes, thank you. It's just there in the door."

Lorraine poured a dollop of cream into the cup, along with the whispered words, '*Mentem Quietam,*' and made a little stirring motion over the cup. The cream swirled down into the coffee without the aid of a spoon.

"Here. You take that and some nice deep breaths, and just sit a moment," Lorraine said gently, handing Shannon the cup.

"Thank you so much," she said sipping. "You know you're right; I don't think I've taken a moment to sit down all morning." She took another, longer drink from her cup. "That hits the spot."

Lorraine smiled gently. "Of course, it does. And what a lovely garden you have! So sunny and bright. Are those azaleas?" She moved around behind Shannon and looked over her shoulder while they spoke the common tongue of gardeners. Once she was sure the quieting spell she'd placed in Shannon's coffee had taken effect and the poor woman's heartbeat had settled to a more relaxed beat, she pulled a pouch from her pocket. She glanced around to make sure nobody had entered the kitchen while they were talking.

"Cheryl said you give piano lessons, how long have you played?"

"Oh, since I was a girl," Shannon said dreamily. "I've always loved the piano . . ."

Lorraine opened the pouch full of spell ingredients she'd prepared the night before, and sparkling powder began to lift itself in a spiral upward. It quickly dissipated into a faintly shimmery glow that faded through the walls and ceiling. For the briefest of seconds, every wall in the house glowed faintly, and then everything went back to normal.

The way Lorraine had explained the spell to us beforehand was that it thinned the veil between our world and others. She said our reality was just one of lots of possible realities existing right next to one another. Communication was sometimes possible, but you often encountered a bad signal. Her spell was like putting a set of rabbit ears on top of the TV. It made the connection clearer. What she didn't realize was just how well it would work.

She resumed her seat next to Shannon, nodding and chuckling at Shannon's description of her first piano teacher.

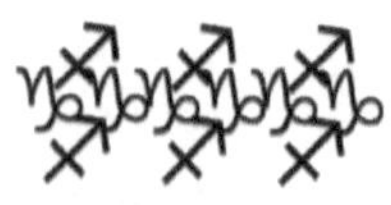

"Jon, do you see that?" David asked, his feet pounding along next to Jon's bike.

"No, where?" Jon asked, looking around. They had nearly completed their search of the neighborhood and were approaching the block where Beth's house sat.

David cocked his head at a house on the upcoming block that was surrounded by a high hedge inside a six-foot chain link fence. The hedge was tidy and evenly groomed, anything else in this cushy neighborhood would have stood out like a sore thumb. It was a large lot. Except for the house on the far corner, it was the only one on that side of the block.

"Wow, even the driveway is gated," Jon mused as he rolled abreast of it. "It must be a pain in the butt to get the car in and out, unless it's automatic . . ." his words trailed off as the gate began rolling open.

"And we have a creeper van!" David hissed. "Call it in, Jon!"

Jon pulled the walkie-talkie off the handlebars and spoke into it quietly, "I think we have a winner!"

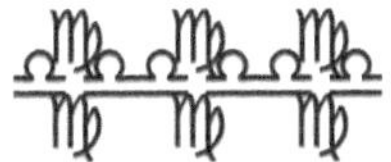

Inside the sewing room, Jen positioned Beth at the table with a pen and a scrap of paper Beth had pulled off her mom's shelf.

"Here's what we're going to do. I'm going to sit in the rocker. Sometimes, if I'm touching something that a ghost has touched, like the letter you gave Crystal, I can see or know things about it, or about the ghost that touched it."

"Coool," Beth said in a low voice. "What should I do?"

"Once it starts, you just ask me to tell you what I'm

seeing. Then you write down whatever I say. Don't worry if it makes any sense or not, and try to write down the exact words, okay?"

"Okay. Are you going into a trance or something? How do I wake you up?"

"Usually, I just wake up on my own, but if I don't, or if I fall out of the chair or anything weird, get my mom, okay? She'll know what to do."

Beth's eyes widened. "Are you sure? Should I go get your mom now?"

"We can if you want to, it's up to you, Beth."

"No, if I did that my mom would come in too, and she'd freak out, and it would be all weird, and we might never figure out what the ghostly lady is trying to tell us. Let's try it. I can do this."

"You're sure?" Jen asked, her fingers touching Beth's shoulder.

"Positive."

"Awesome. Okay. Here goes." Jen seated herself carefully in the rocker.

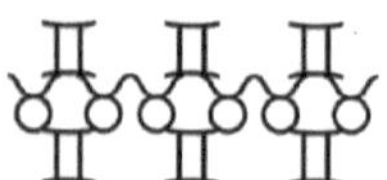

In the dark, cold basement, Desiree shivered and pulled her knees up against her chest. The polo shirt and pleated skirt that made up her school uniform, although plenty warm enough for Thursday's sunshine and 70-degree weather, down here were sadly insufficient. She didn't have a watch, and the basement windows were nearly all covered with heavy black paper, so the only sliver of light that came into the room was where the paper had come away on one side of the window above her head.

It was through this thin slice of window Crystal caught sight of the blue chair sitting just outside. A blue chair, with a curve, a rocking chair? Maybe. That and the tiny beam of light it let in was what she had to hold tight to.

She was still cursing herself for falling for that jerk, Jason's play. She knew he was trouble, but those big brown eyes just sucked her in. He'd sweet-talked her into stepping inside his garage to smoke a joint. She hadn't even really wanted the joint, just to make him think she was cool enough to know how. She'd sure seen her mom smoke them often enough. She and Crystal had even sneaked some puffs when their mom wasn't home.

This stuff wasn't like what she remembered though. After her first puff, Desiree had felt woozy and needed to sit down. Jason, so gentlemanly, had pulled a lawn chair over and taken her hand so she could sit. The last thing she remembered was the sound of his garage door rattling down, and vaguely, through the open door to the kitchen, the sound of his voice on the telephone.

"Got another one for you. Yeah. Just bring the van over, and we'll move her now."

She'd awakened inside a cage.

Desiree scooted a little closer to the side of the cage that met with the one to her left. It was too dark to see how many cages had been built in this dank little basement room, but she knew there were at least three because that's how many girls had down here until just a little while ago.

The cages were about four feet square, and only about four feet high; not enough room to stand up or stretch out. They had to crawl. Each cell had a bucket, a plastic bottle full of tepid water, and a poncho liner that, although thin, was at least warm.

The girl on her left's name was Maria, but that was about as much information as Desiree had gotten out of her. Maria didn't speak any English, and Desiree's Spanish was limited to *hola, taco* and *burrito*. She figured they were about the same age, maybe eleven or twelve. She had managed to pantomime to Desiree that they shouldn't drink from the water bottles. She couldn't explain why, but Desiree figured it out pretty quickly when the third girl took a drink and immediately passed out. The water was drugged with something.

The third girl was maybe a little bit older, but she was, what Beth's mom would call, *simple*. Desiree's mom would have called her *retarded*, but that just sounded mean, Des thought. Desiree had tried to talk to her at first, but the conversation went nowhere fast. She found out her name, Missy, and that she wanted to go home, and that was about it. Missy was too scared to stop crying, and then once she took a big drink of her water, she fell asleep with her scrap of blanket wrapped around her head and her thumb stuffed into her mouth.

Sometime in the night, she'd been taken away.

She and Maria watched it happen. The door to their room was pushed open, a shaft of light, almost blinding after all the darkness, shot through the opening. A slight man unlocked the door to Missy's cage and then stood aside while Jason, that rotten creep, crouched down and caught hold of Missy by the ankle. Missy never even woke up. He dragged her out of the cage and out the door, then slammed it shut. Desiree heard a lock click on the outside. The whole process took less than thirty seconds.

Then she heard voices.

"I'm going to have to make an extra trip. My buyer only wants this one. The other two will have to wait until

Miller comes through on his next pass."

"How long?"

"Forty-eight hours."

"Shit. Okay. Let's get dummy here up the stairs." Desiree thought she recognized Jason's voice. "Come on sweet thing. You're going to meet your new papa."

Then they heard the sounds of scuffling and a door slamming.

Then silence, and darkness.

Desiree felt the tears burning down her cheeks. If it weren't for the dreams about the ghost lady from Beth's house, Desiree thought she might have freaked out already. To be truthful, she wasn't really sure if they were dreams or not. It was pretty hard to tell after a while in the dark if you were awake or asleep, and since she hadn't had anything to eat since lunch at school on Thursday, everything was starting to feel a little wonky.

But in the dreams, if that's what they were, the ghost lady came and held her. She stroked her head and rocked her. Desiree thought once she heard music.

It was after Missy got taken away that the ghost brought a pen and paper, and pushed them into Desiree's hands, whispering what sounded like, *Sister! Tell sister! You write. I cannot.* She lay her almost translucent hands over Desiree's and whispered again, *Write!* So, Desiree wrote.

> *Jason, the motorcycle guy, tricked*
> *me into coming into his garage. I'm*
> *locked in a basement and it's so dark &*
> *scary in here! All I can see out the win-*
> *dow is a blue rocker on the porch.*
> *There were two other girls here but one*
> *got taken away. I'm afraid we're next! I*

*think the house ghost is helping me but
I don't know and I'm so scared, please
Cryssybel please help me!*

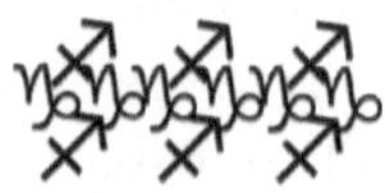

Jen sat down in the rocker in the sewing room. For a few seconds, nothing happened. Jen looked at Beth's face, so bright and excited and saw her eyes widen, staring at the arm of the chair under Jen's hand. Jenny had a bare second to recognize it as one of Lorraine's spells, before she was sucked down into a silent pool.

Beth saw the flash and looked to Jenny to say something, and realized that Jenny was already deep in her trance, or whatever it was that was happening. Beth had a moment of panic and almost screamed for their moms, but then remembered what she was supposed to do.

"What is it, Jenny? What do you see?" she asked, in a voice that cracked with nerves.

Jenny sat up very straight in the chair and folded her hands primly in her lap. She gave herself a little shake and looked around wide eyed. Then she turned and focused on Beth.

"Child, listen carefully! There's no time. Your sister has been taken by evil men. If you and the others don't get to her right away, she'll be lost to you forever!"

Beth stared at Jen. She was a smart kid. She understood instinctively that this wasn't Jenny speaking; that somehow, she was talking to her house ghost instead, and she didn't waste any time with foolish questions.

"Where is she?!"

The amazing ghost of this lovely woman who had

been brutally killed in her own home and ruthlessly stolen away from her own children, used the strength of Lorraine's magic and Jenny's gifts to stand up out of the chair, turn to the window, sweep aside the curtains and point.

From this window, because their house was on a little rise, they could see right down into the back yard across the way. There, next to the blue rocking lawn chair was the locked cellar door.

"There!" she shouted.

Then every light in Beth's house started flashing madly on and off. Every faucet turned on and boiling hot and icy cold water rushed out. Every TV set and radio turned on with the volume up as high as it could go. The sound of glass breaking from other rooms reached them. Fabric and patterns flew off shelves and Jenny collapsed to the floor.

"Beth!" she hissed. "Go get my mom!"

Beth rushed for the kitchen, just as the screaming began in the living room.

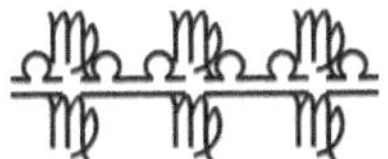

Mr. Rakow didn't even have time to respond to Jon's message before we all nearly collided at the corner.

"Right there, Mr. Rakow. Tall hedge, panel van, locked gate," David rattled off, barely even short of breath. "Gate just opened; van should be pulling out any second."

"Good work, boys! Circle around the block to the east side, see if you can spot a way over the hedge. We'll keep on this way and meet you on the far side.

"Roger, Sar'nt!" David snapped a hasty salute, and the two of them peeled off around the block, the way we had just come.

"C'mon Angie. Let's see what we can see."

My adrenaline had amped up. I tried to stay chill, but I had a feeling about this. One that was confirmed by the increased warmth of the blue stone that hung from the leather cord around my neck. I glanced at David. The green stone he wore was also glowing faintly. We were definitely on to something here.

The front of the house in question was pretty effectively concealed by trees, native flowers and a scattering of tall, decorative prairie grasses that filled the pocket-sized front yard. It was a landscape that, although meticulously kept, was designed to obscure, rather than reveal the house. It also looked unused, as if all of the coming and going happened from the garage to the side of the house, behind the tall fence, and even taller hedge.

I heard the clunk of the gate mechanism rumbling, and the driveway was revealed just as Mr. Rakow and Shadow reached it. He had quickened their pace to reach that spot in time and now slowed down to get as much of a look inside as we could in the few short steps it would take us to walk past the opening.

Shadow seemed to pick up on his strategy and became exceedingly interested in the bush growing at the corner of the driveway. He sniffed, and sniffed some more. Alesta one-upped her new mentors and decided it was the perfect place to stop and deposit a poop.

While Mr. Rakow dug in his many pockets searching for a plastic bag, I angled myself so I could get a good view of the man in question.

He had opened the passenger door of his van and was lifting in two little old dogs. He was a slight man, not dangerous looking in the least. Quite to the contrary, he appeared pale and unassuming; a pale, middle-aged guy, with tired brown hair that was thin and beginning to gray, dressed in faded khaki pants, a light-colored polo shirt and a gray Members Only jacket. His feet were clad in loafers. There was absolutely nothing memorable or re-markable about him. He was practically invisible.

Shadow and Alesta clearly did not agree. Every mus-cle in Shadow's body was tensed. He wasn't pulling at his leash or anything, it would have been very easy for any-one unfamiliar with his subtle alert stance to have missed it, but all my alarm bells were sounding, and it seemed Alesta's were too.

Mr. Rakow made a business of cleaning up after Alesta, making sure no trace was left behind. The pale man closed the passenger door of his van with a secure but gentle thump and walked around behind it to get to the driver's side. As he approached us, he spared me a glance and then looked appreciatively at the dogs.

When Mr. Rakow straightened up, the man ad-dressed him.

"Beautiful Shepherds."

Mr. Rakow nodded noncommittally.

"How old is the pup?" the pale man asked.

"Not sure, exactly. She's a rescue. Nearly six months," Mr. Rakow replied easily.

Mr. Rakow might be a little high strung, but he was a pretty smooth operator when the situation called for it. I tried to control my thudding heart. I wasn't at all sure how this man was dangerous, but the closer he got to where we stood, the more nervous I felt.

"Well then," the pale man said, his voice light and casual. "Have a nice walk."

Mr. Rakow nodded in return, and we continued past

the open gate.

Alesta's eyes were trained on Shadow. I set my happily clueless face on high beam and gaped around, doing my best to absorb everything I could see while still looking totally harmless. Two could play at that game.

Shadow stayed firmly at Mr. Rakow's heel, and Alesta did her best to copy. I kept her leash pretty short. I wasn't sure Shadow wouldn't discover some totally valid excuse to whirl around and behead this guy before he got into the driver's side of the van, and if he did, I was convinced Alesta would follow suit.

I got a pretty decent look at as much of the house that was visible, along with the garage and a portion of the back yard. The pale man's little dogs happily discovered something to yap about, and when I glanced back that direction, a flash of movement caught my eye.

It was from a window in the house up the hill — the curtains had been flung wide open, and I could see the silhouette of a woman, or maybe a girl, pointing right at us.

And then we were past the driveway.

That window, I wondered, was that — "Mr. Rakow, can we see Beth's house from here?"

"Let's see, it's on a little rise, it should be — yes, there. That's it right there," he said, pointing. Right at the house with the flapping curtain.

"Mr. Rakow!" I started.

Then Mr. Rakow's walkie-talkie crackled again.

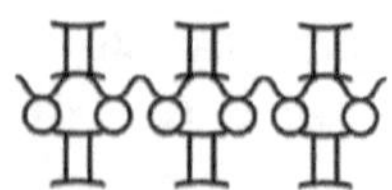

Barb and Crystal got a ride to the shopping center

just at the edge of the neighborhood and walked from there. Just as they were approaching the block Barb recalled from the map that should take them to the house, they caught sight of a tall, thin guy running out of his house at top speed.

"What's that about?" Barb asked.

"Something feels wrong," Crystal said, frowning worriedly.

"He looks like an asshole. Let's take a look." Barb said.

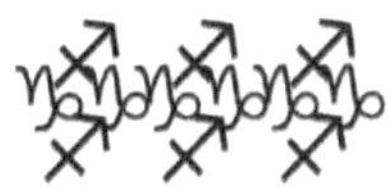

All hell had broken loose in Beth's house. Jen was struggling to get to her feet in the sewing room, and Beth was running full tilt down the long hallway toward the kitchen. Thumps and crashes were coming from the living room, and someone was screaming.

"Mom! Mom! Mom!" Beth shouted, barreling towards the kitchen.

Lorraine and Shannon shared a panicked look before Lorraine leapt to her feet shouting, "Call 911! Now!" and rushed toward the sound of the ruckus.

In the living room, Alan and Beth's brother Matt were on their feet. In the corner of the room, a terrifying black hole had opened in the floor, and the side table, lamp and most of the rug were already mostly sucked down into the abyss. Bolts of electricity shot from the lamp that was still mostly plugged in and a foul wind swirled and blasted from the hole.

Lorraine snatched both boys by the backs of their collars and dragged them backward out of the room.

"What the hell is going on?" screamed Matt above the din.

"Get back!" yelled Lorraine. "Get out! Out the kitchen door! Take Shannon! Go now!" She shoved them both in the direction of the kitchen.

Beth rocketed into the room just then only to be snagged by the arm by Lorraine and swung around, away from the chaos.

"Where's my daughter?" Lorraine demanded.

"This way! Come with me!" shouted Beth, sparing a terrified glance at the living room and then turning to drag Lorraine back the way they'd come.

Jen had managed to get to her feet by the time Beth dragged Lorraine into the sewing room. Lights were still flashing, music was blaring, and the second they entered the room, Shannon's sewing machine fired up and started running at full tilt the shining needle pounding up and down ferociously, biting into nothingness.

"Jenny!" Lorraine cried out.

"Beth!" Jen yelled. "Tell my mom what you saw!"

Lorraine grabbed Beth by the shoulders and pulled her close. Straining for calm, she asked, "What did you see, Beth?"

"The ghost! She came and talked with Jenny's mouth! She said Desiree was there!" Beth ran to the window and pointed. Lorraine dodged past the whirring sewing machine and looked. From her vantage point, she could not only see the house with the blue rocking chairs in the back, but also me, staring through the open gate as we walked past the driveway.

"Come on, girls! We have to get out of here," she spun and made a run for the door, pushing Jenny and Beth ahead of her.

They looked down the hallway toward the living

room and made the instantaneous group decision to go the opposite direction. The darkness and wind had increased in ferocity. Family pictures were flying off the walls of the hallway, shattering against the hardwood floor. There was glass everywhere.

"This way!" Beth yelled. "We can get out this way!"

Jen and Lorraine followed her down the hall and through the master bedroom. At the far end was a set of French doors leading out to the back yard. The three of them raced through, barely making it past the giant dresser before it flung itself down, the big mirror on top exploding into a million sharp, glittery pieces.

"Go go go!" Lorraine urged, half supporting Jen who was still swaying unsteadily from her full-on ghost takeover experience.

Beth maneuvered the locks on the French doors as well as she could with books and pillows and rolls of spare toilet paper from the master bath flying at her at approximately a million miles an hour. And then, they were outside. Shannon rushed over and grabbed Beth in a huge embrace.

"Baby! You're all right!"

"I'm okay, Mom. Are you?"

"Yes! I called 911, and they're on their way. What in God's name is going on in there?" she cried out her arms around both of her kids, plus Alan. Beth hugged her back and ran over to where Jen was sprawled on the grass, rapidly filling Lorraine in on what had occurred in the sewing room.

Meanwhile, Lorraine was patting down the pockets of her long leather vest. It was the one I loved with the fringe and the beads. I'd tried it on secretly once when she was out. I hoped someday when I was grown, I'd have one just like it. It had masses of pockets, big deep ones. Lorraine always said she loved it because when she wore it, she didn't have to carry a purse.

From the bottom of one of those deep pockets, with shaking hands, she finally drew out what she was searching for — her walkie-talkie.

"Rakow! The house! It's the one you're right by, with the tall hedge. That's it. Blue rockers! Not blue rocks! We can see them from here! Blue rockers by the cellar door! There's a padlock on it; gotta be a big one if I can see it from here."

"Roger, Lorraine," Mr. Rakow responded. *"Are you all right?"*

"Really no, but we're safe for now. I think. Can you get in?"

"We're on it, Mom!" came Jon's voice over the third walkie. *"David's found a way in. Do you need help?"*

Jen reached up and tapped Lorraine's elbow, motioning that she should hand over the walkie. Her red stone was glowing hotly on its leather cord. Lorraine glanced down and handed it over. Jen took a visible second to gather her words, clicked the button on the walkie and said, "Two things. Number one, *men*. Plural. Men took Desiree. Watch your backs. Number two, *no time*. Get your butt in there, Owens. I know what you're thinking. Do it. Now. And put Angie on."

Mr. Rakow handed me the walkie. *"I'm here, Jen."*

"Crystal and Barb are on their way. They need you and Alesta. Keep your eyes wide open, Ang. You'll know what to do."

"Got it," I responded. *Crap*, I thought. I hated vague prophecy. I preferred detailed plans. With bullet points and colored highlights. Oh well. Eyes wide open. I thought about what Phyllida's magic book had said.

Beware the grayness; it is far more dangerous than it appears.

The girl has one foot in the country of Lost, and one foot firmly planted here, but not for long. She needs her defender to anchor her. You must hurry, child. Before the sun falls tomorrow, she will be beyond your help. Use the enchantment on this page to open your eyes so you may see past the grayness. Do not fail, child. This girl holds the key.

Mr. Rakow and I had rounded the corner and spotted David and Jon near the fence along the east side of the pale man's property. The hedge was just as high and thick here, I couldn't tell what David had found, but he was excited. We rushed toward them.

"I can get in, right here." David pointed at a place where a tiny gap in the hedge revealed a structure on the other side of the fence. "There's a shed right there. If you give me a leg up, I can do this."

That much of the plan was solid.

"What about once you get inside? Lorraine said there was a big padlock on the cellar door."

"I don't know, but there must be a way. Jen said she knew what I was thinking and that I should get my butt in there, so there *must* be a way."

"Look inside the shed, kid," interjected Mr. Rakow. "Once you get over the fence. All kinds of stuff in a man's shed, maybe bolt cutters, or a hack saw. Maybe even a spare key."

"Yes! You're a genius. Now somebody boost me up."

"What if he comes back?" I said. Somebody had to say it.

"Distraction!" David and Jon exclaimed in unison.

"Take the walkie!" I handed him the one I held, leaving me, Jon and Mr. Rakow with the other.

Mr. Rakow crouched with his hands cupped. David took a step back and eyed his target.

"On three," he looked at Mr. Rakow. "One, two three!" David took two steps at a run, stepped into Mr. Rakow's hand and jumped. With Mr. Rakow's added boost, he almost made it over like a hurdler, just barely grazing the fence with one foot, and the hedge with one arm as he tumbled over onto the shed roof.

We couldn't, however, see the landing. He must have rolled because he didn't break anything that time.

"I'm in!"

"You two hit that corner and stand watch. Take Alesta. Let David know immediately if you see the van returning, or anything else. I'll stay out of sight here."

"How do we alert you if he comes back?"

"Whistle."

"Yes sir!" Jon and I responded, and with one backward look at the hedge, we scrambled for the corner.

Jon, Alesta and I got to the corner and crossed the street to where we had a 360-degree line of sight on anyone approaching the driveway or the house, and then . . . stopped. Yikes. It's seriously not easy to go from super-excitement-pumping-adrenaline mode to guard duty in two seconds flat.

Alesta didn't seem to have much trouble with it. Once she determined that we were parked for the moment, she flopped down in the grass in the sunshine, tongue lolling and tail thumping the ground. I perched on the retaining wall surrounding the pretty yellow house on the corner, scanning straight and to my left. Jon positioned himself opposite me and sat astride his bike, scanning the other two directions.

Jon's energy returned to its usual low-key vibe pretty quickly. His absolute lack of curiosity never ceased to amaze me. There he sat on his bike in the sunshine, scanning the street for a creeper van, identified for us by a ghost, to protect our best friend who was breaking and entering the creep's house to save a kidnap victim like it was the most unremarkable thing in the world.

"Say," he said abruptly. "Did you have Mrs. Rogge last year for Algebra?"

"I did," I responded, a little surprised. Small talk wasn't usually part of Jon's repertoire. And math never ever was.

Jon rocked back and forth on his bike a little bit. Slow motion fidgeting on wheels. I continued my scanning.

"I have her next year. I hear she's pretty tough. What did you think?" he asked, completely casually.

I raised my eyebrows at him and shrugged. "She's hardcore on turning homework in on time, but she's also great if you have any questions." Math wasn't my strongest suit. I was in the advanced track, but I struggled. I always had lots of questions.

"What electives are you going to take in 9th?" he asked, leaning down to scratch a mosquito bite on his calf.

"My elective periods always get used up with music classes. Orchestra and Concert Band, plus Mr. Quick wants us to keep up the quartet. How about you?"

Sirens wailed in the distance.

"I was thinking about taking an art class," he replied. "I was planning on taking shop, but Mr. Andrews is such a jerk, I don't feel like putting up with his bull for a whole year."

"Good call," I responded. The shop teacher's reputation was so awful, even I knew about it. "What about woodworking? Isn't that with Mr. Shelby? He's pretty okay."

"Oh yeah, that might be cool."

Jon looked at me then and smiled. My heart very unexpectedly skipped a beat. My cheeks flushed hotly, and I turned away, hoping like crazy he hadn't noticed.

That's when I caught sight of Barb and Crystal coming around the corner off Cotner onto this little side street. Directly opposite them, was our troublemaking Chachi, jogging around his corner toward the pale man's gate.

"Crap!" I said.

"It gets worse," Jon said laconically. I turned to look. The van was making its way toward us. It was about three blocks away.

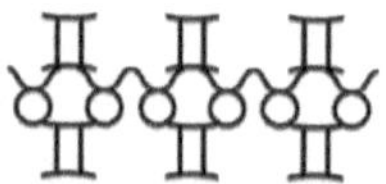

In Barb's backyard, Jen dropped the walkie-talkie and looked at Lorraine. "It was the spell, right? Thinning the veil? It allowed Mrs. O'Shea to talk through me, but it let her killer's energy pass through, too."

"I think that about sums it up," Lorraine replied tersely. "I think the murder site must have opened a portal of some kind. I was really not expecting that."

"Can we close it?" Jen asked.

"Maybe. I'd need a power boost, though," Lorraine said, her face screwed up in concentration.

"I thought you'd say that. I think we can tap into that one," Jen tilted her head over to where Shannon was crouched protectively near Beth, Matt, and Alan. They were shaky, pale, and praying. Their hands were joined, and they were reciting something, maybe a rosary, Jen wasn't sure.

"Oof, really?" Lorraine looked skeptical. "Do you think we should?"

The roof of Beth's house caved in.

"Yes. I think we should," Jen replied, calmly. "Now."

"Ok, kid. Just like we practiced. Only without our nice safe house, and our friendly coven—"

"Mom!"

"Okay!"

Jen started chanting the spell that would let her act as a conduit for the energy being produced and received by the prayers of the faithful four crouched over by the swing set. It was a simple enough spell, one that Lorraine's coven often made use of when they wanted to pool their powers. With all of our supernatural adventuring, Lorraine had been forced into using more and more powerful spells, and one person, one witch, only had so much power at her command. Magic, like everything else we did, was a group effort.

Beth and her family obviously weren't witches, but the power of belief was much of a muchness, regardless of what tradition it drew from. Positive psychic energy was positive psychic energy, and that's what Lorraine needed.

Lorraine drew herself up and held her arms out. Not all binding spells were as complicated as the one she'd used on Charlie at the school. That one took complexity and finesse. This one was basically a sledgehammer.

She took a deep breath, her hair and all the fringe on her leather vest standing nearly straight up with the power gathered all in one place. "I bind thee! I bind thee! I bind thee!" She spoke in a low, loud, rumbling tone. On her final word, she let fly, and all the energy she'd gathered went charging at the house like a locomotive.

BOOM!

It sounded like a crazy loud sonic boom, and then, sudden silence. All the chaos coming from inside quieted, just as the fire trucks and police cars came screaming up the street.

Lorraine collapsed down in the grass next to Jen. She lay there, breathing heavily for a moment, then raised herself on one elbow. She eyed Jen and held up one hand. Jen high-fived her, and they both fell back into the grass, smiling.

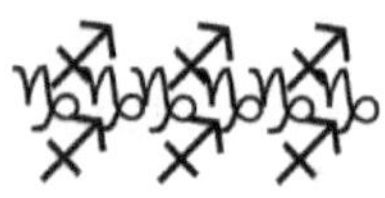

I grabbed the walkie-talkie. I needed to alert David, but the sirens I'd heard a minute ago were getting louder.

"Crap! Are they going to Beth's house?"

BOOM!

All at once, my necklace blazed with color. Everything in my sight became blindingly blue for a second, and then it was gone.

"What the hell was that?" I yelled.

"That felt like Mom!" Jon yelled back.

There was absolutely zero time for me to focus on the fact that this appeared to be the moment Jon shed his umbrella of practiced disinterest and admitted that he'd been paying attention to absolutely everything the whole time. Or that he had really pretty eyes. ARGH! No time!

My ears ringing and my thoughts racing, I yelled into the walkie, "David! David! Can you hear me, over? Jen, report! The van is nearly back to the house! I repeat, the van is coming and the second man is at the gate!"

No response from anyone. The van kept coming.

"Get ready," Jon called out.

"For what?" I demanded, eyes wide.

"Distraction!"

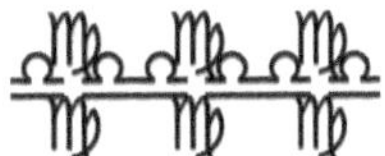

Barb and Crystal turned the same direction as the running guy and spied Angie and one of her friends at the end of the block. Just then, BOOM! Some kind of crazy sonic boom rattled the windows in all the houses on the block.

"What the hell?" Crystal asked, eyes wide, holding her hands over her ears.

Angie's weirdo friend took off into the middle of the street and started doing some kind of bike circus tricks right in front of a van that was barreling down the street. Angie turned toward them and shouted, pointing at the running dude, "Barb! Stop him! He's the one! Don't let him go in there!"

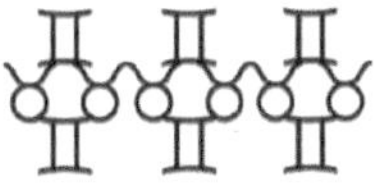

After crouching by the shed for a long moment, scanning the property for any signs of life, David busted the flimsy catch on the shed door and stuck his head inside. It was nicely organized, and reasonably clean. Immediately to his left was a flashlight, which he snagged and beamed around to inspect the shed's contents.

Lawnmower, rakes, sprinkler attachments, two hoses neatly looped and hung on nails on the wall, endless small garden implements all hung neatly on a pegboard.

"C'mon, man," David whispered. "You've got everything but the kitchen sink in here. Give me what I need." Unconsciously, he put his hand on his stone. Just then, BOOM! The shed shook. A blast of green light erupted from his necklace. It knocked him back, and he had to hang on to the doorway of the shed to keep from falling over. "What the hell?" he muttered. He righted himself and beamed the flashlight around again. There. On the far wall, with handles that must have been a yard long, hung a brand new, heavy duty bolt cutter.

David rubbed his necklace, whispered, "thank you," grabbed the bolt cutter and tore across the lawn to the cellar door. The padlock was no competition for the right tool, and David had the lock off and the doors torn open in a jiffy. He flitted down the stairs to the door at the bottom. It was locked.

"Crap!" he hissed. This was no padlock situation, but a regular door with a key. The hinges were on the inside, so he couldn't remove the pins and just lift the door out of the way. He rubbed his stone again. Jen had foreseen him getting through this obstacle course, so there had to be a way.

He peered at the lock: old door, big keyhole. One of the old-timey skeleton keys, he guessed. Everybody's grandma had at least one of them in her junk drawer in case one of the kids got locked in the bathroom. They were everywhere, he thought. As common as air.

At that exact second, a whiff of breeze lifted his sweaty hair, and he heard a little chime. He turned toward the noise. It came from above his head. He lifted the flashlight and beamed it up over the door lintel. Hanging from a string on a nail above the door, clinking musically against the frame, hung the key.

Wasting no time, he grabbed it and unlocked the door. The basement was dark but clean and orderly. To his right were the stairs leading up to the house. Straight ahead were shelves full of canned goods and a few boxes. To his left was a locked door.

"Bingo!" he crowed quietly. "Desiree? Are you in there?" The key to this lock hung right outside the door. Apparently, the pale man wasn't worried about anyone getting in, just about his prisoners getting out. David unlocked the door and shone his light into the little room. What he saw made him angry to the roots of his soul.

The room reeked of filth. The girls' buckets hadn't been emptied in two days, and the stench hung heavily in the room. Two girls, pale and dirty, blinked back at him. One scooted away from him, terror in her eyes. The other one, the one in the school uniform came forward.

"Did my sister send you? Did Crystal get my message?"

"Yes! She and Barb asked us to help. C'mon, let's get you out of here." He used the bolt cutters to cut the locks off both cages and backed up to give them room to crawl out.

"This is Maria. She doesn't speak any English," said Desiree.

"I'm David. Come on, let's go. My friends are outside, but we have to be quiet. *Silencio.* Come on." They crept up the stairs and sped across the yard to the shed. David pulled out the walkie-talkie and clicked the talk button.

"I've got them. We're out of the house."

Nothing. The walkie was dead.

He rushed over to the hedge where he'd left Mr.

Rakow waiting out of sight. "Mr. Rakow!" he hissed. "Mr. Rakow?"

Nothing.

My head whipped from Barb and Crystal to Chachi, to Jon, to the oncoming van.

"Crap!"

Jon rode his bike out into the middle of the intersection and started doing some of the asinine bike tricks he'd been learning from his long-haired bike-punk friend, Todd.

"Hey Angie, look at me!" he crowed, popping wheelies and bouncing around on his back wheel, right out in the path of the oncoming van.

"Jon, no! That's insane! Cut it out, man!"

"Take care of him, Ang!" growled Jon, pointing over at the corner where the pale man's stooge, pretty boy Chachi was almost to the gate.

Behind Jon, the van accelerated.

"No!!" I rushed toward Jon, screaming over my shoulder and pointing, "Barb! Stop him! He's the one! Don't let him go in there!"

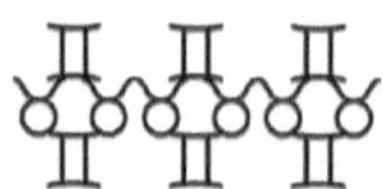

From the far end of the block, Barb heard Angie, and grinned savagely. "Oh yeah. I knew this baby was going to come in handy. I just knew it." She loaded three ball bearings into the pouch of the wrist rocket she had already bound to her right arm. Barb pulled back, aimed and let fly.

Direct hit. She'd knocked the jerk right off his feet. He lay on the sidewalk screaming and cussing.

"What now?" Crystal asked.

"Now, I reload," Barb replied, grinning.

Jon bounced from the front to the back wheel of his bike and executed some complicated spin that took him slightly away from the center of the intersection when the van cruised through, and then I heard the horrifying sounds I'd been praying not to hear.

THUD, CRUNCH and brakes squealing.

Followed immediately by the sound of Chachi screaming like a stuck pig, and the sound of Barb crowing with laughter.

My lips were too dry to whistle. I ran for Jon.

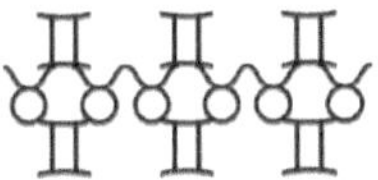

I flew around the front of the van, past the pale man before I even realized he was out of the vehicle, and knelt at Jon's side. He wasn't moving. His bike was mangled under the front wheels, but Jon must have been thrown clear. He lay on his back a few yards away from the van, blood running from under his head — too much blood.

My conscious brain went into shock when I saw that. Anything else I did after that moment was purely the product of dumb luck, magic, divine intervention, or more likely, all of the above.

I remember reaching out for him, thinking, I shouldn't move him, but reaching for him anyway, and touching his cheek. I remember feeling like I weighed no more than an atom, that I had no body, just energy, and eyes. Wide open eyes. I remember seeing the crack in his skull, but the perspective was all skewed. I wasn't seeing it from where I crouched over him, but from behind and from inside and from above. I could see where all the pieces should fit back together, and I could see a creeping grayness seeping in between the cracks. Something about that grayness terrified me in a primal way. Phyllida's words came to me, *Beware the grayness.* My heart thudded in my hears. I reached my hand out. Blue light rolled off my fingers and into all the cracks and crevasses, pushing the creeping grayness away and bringing the pieces back together, binding, healing — covering everything in peaceful blue light.

For a second, nothing happened. I held my breath. And then, Jon's eyes popped open, and he blinked up at me. "Hey Ang, did it work? Did we stop him?"

And then there was the sound of Mr. Rakow's shoulder hitting the pale man in the gut and knocking him to the street where Shadow waited, teeth bared.

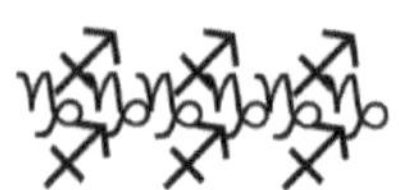

Shadow didn't get to eat the pale man. Before Mr. Rakow executed his pro-level tackle, he'd actually flagged down one of the police cruisers that had responded to the multiple reports that got called in, neighbors reporting everything from possible fire, tornado or full-fledged Armageddon at Beth's house.

At this point it should surprise nobody that the officer driving the police car Mr. Rakow just happened to wave over was Officer Yardley, our neighborhood cop.

He always seemed to be on hand any time we had cases that intersected with law enforcement.

Officer Yardley was right behind Mr. Rakow and was able to cuff the pale man before Shadow got a chance to do much more than menace him.

Shadow was sorely disappointed.

While Barb kept Chachi, aka Jason, occupied until another officer could arrive, Crystal ran to the pale man's gate and wrestled it open with a little help from David on the other side. Once they got it open, Crystal and Desiree fell into each other's arms and stayed that way, I believe, for the rest of that long day.

It all got pretty confusing. There were a lot of people milling around. A Spanish speaking officer arrived and listened to Maria's story of being lured into a van and waking up in a cage. Within a half an hour, a blue station wagon arrived, and a couple with several kids piled out and took possession of Maria amid a great deal of crying and laughing and translating.

A different officer brought Shannon over from the house and took statements from everyone while they hugged and cried with joy and relief that the lost had been found.

Lorraine and Jen arrived and promptly left again with the ambulance. Jon had his head X-rayed six ways from Sunday that afternoon. There were no fractures, no bumps, bruises, contusions. No headache, no blurry vision. Not even any gravel in his hair. He was perfectly fine, except for the stain on the back his shirt where the blood had pooled.

It turned out that the pale man and Jason were the first crack in a case Officer Yardley and his partner Officer Citta had been working on for months. They would go on to uncover a portion of a nation-wide human trafficking market that had been flourishing in secrecy in the Midwest for decades, picking off vulnerable kids to be used either as field labor or in the sex trades. Since Interstate 80 runs through Lincoln and Omaha, they were convenient stops along a route that ran from coast to coast.

Once the crowds began to thin out, I caught sight of Barb standing with Mr. Rakow. They were chatting, and petting the dogs. Alesta looked at Barb the same way Shadow looked at Mr. Rakow. I sighed a little, not much really, but a little. It was her. It had been her from the first. I walked over to join them.

"That was one hell of a shot, Barb," I said. "You nailed that guy from across the street; took him down in one. Nicely done!"

"Thanks for giving me a chance to help. It felt good to get one back on the slime that kidnapped Desiree."

"So, what's your plan from here? Do you want a ride back to Whitehall?" Mr. Rakow asked.

"No, I don't think I'll be going back there," Barb said thoughtfully.

I looked at her then and saw something I wasn't expecting to see. It wasn't exactly like what I saw when I knelt next to Jon when he was hurt, but it was the same kind of seeing. I saw Barb, but instead of being surrounded by gracious, suburban homes in a neighborhood in the eastern third of Nebraska, I was seeing her standing defiantly in an arid wilderness. I saw her armed with a sword and a bow, trekking through a darkened landscape. And next to her I saw Alesta, her defender.

Mr. Rakow and I drove them out to the south edge of town, but not until we'd stopped by his place and provisioned them both for a journey of some length. Among the things he packed in her backpack were a compass, a compact book of laminated maps, like the ones used in

Army field duty, and a picture of Shadow, along with all of our phone numbers.

We dropped them off on a gravel road near the furthest south entrance to Wilderness Park. We said our goodbyes and got back in the car.

"Will they be okay?" I asked.

Mr. Rakow pointed, and at the top of the hill Barb was climbing, illuminated by the fire of the setting sun I saw the figure of a white haired woman. I couldn't see her face, but I knew her. She was the Grandmother, owner of the apothecary cabinet and gifter of Phyllida's book. She held her arms out to Barb and knelt to stroke Alesta's nose.

Travelers, I thought. They disappeared together over the rise.

I didn't see any of them again in Lincoln for a long time.

Epilogue

Sunday afternoon found the three of us camped out on the big sofa in the basement at Jen's vegging and watching reruns of MASH and Perry Mason. I'd spent the night, so in truth, we hadn't moved far from this spot since the night before.

Jon wasn't there; he'd gone to the movies with his buddy Todd and Todd's girlfriend, Jade. I was kind of relieved about that, actually. I had a lot of complicated feelings competing for space inside my head about Jon at the moment.

Jen and David had been pretty quiet about the whole, me saving Jon's life with magic thing. Once Jon and Jen and Lorraine had gotten back from the hospital after getting Jon checked out, Lorraine had a long talk with Mr. Rakow who had seen the whole thing go down from just a few yards away.

Mr. Rakow understood that Jon's (incredibly dumb) plan was to *pretend* to be hit. He had circled around the front and was aiming to get in its blind spot and kick the side of the van, loud enough to spook the pale man into thinking he'd hit him so he'd stop.

Griess was the pale man's name, we'd learned. Mr. Griess.

What Jon hadn't anticipated, was that Mr. Griess would *actually* hit him. And he had. Very deliberately. I'd seen him accelerate. So had Mr. Rakow.

It turned out, Mr. Griess had gotten a message on his beeper from Chachi, aka Jason. Part of Jason's job was to guard the house while Griess was out, and he had spotted David making his run across the yard, carrying the bolt cutters. He sent Mr. Griess a series of beeper messages and then tore out of his place to go and confront David.

Thank goodness Barb and Crystal had been right there, and that Barb had come prepared with the wrist rocket and kickass aim.

Griess and Jason used some numeric codes on their beepers, a sort of shorthand mashup of police 20-codes and upside-down text formed from numbers. It didn't take Officer Yardley much time to crack it, and that was what gave the police the evidence they needed to show that the two were in cahoots, that Jason had access to the property, and that Mr. Griess knew the intruder was, specifically, a "boy" spelled out on the beeper as an upside down "409".

When Griess saw Jon, he assumed that *he* was the boy who had broken in and had tried to silence him. Permanently.

Griess hadn't counted on Jen just happening to be plugged into a major magical power source right then, or the connection between the three of us and our necklaces, or the fact that all of that would soup-up Phyllida's spell and allow me not only to see exactly where Jon was injured but then let me, heal him, somehow, some way.

Once Lorraine had gotten Mr. Rakow's story, and Officer Yardley's, she'd come into Jen's room where we were getting ready for bed, and she'd hugged me. Really hard. For a long time. I'm pretty sure she was crying, but all she said was, "Thank you, Angie girl. Thank you for what you did."

It was all kind of heavy.

By late Sunday afternoon, after hours and hours of brain numbing TV, David flopped onto his back on the beanbag chair next to the couch and groaned. "Angie, are you about finished over-thinking this? Because this mopey silence thing is getting really old."

"I'm not mopey," I grunted mopily.

"Bull puckey!" Jen retorted.

"Jeez, okay you guys," I said defensively.

"Look, Ang." Jen reached over and took my chin in her hand. She stared me right in the eyes. "If Jon was going to die for real, don't you think I'd have foreseen it? He is my twin, after all."

"Probably," I admitted.

"And if I'd seen that, don't you think I'd have warned you?"

"Well, yeah. You would have."

"And I didn't, right?" Hand still gripping my chin, she made me shake and then nod my head.

"Right," I conceded.

"Which means what?" She squeezed my cheeks so that I was making a fish face.

"Oooommmm," I said between squished fish lips. "That he wasn't going to die?"

"Exactly!" she exclaimed, letting go of my face and bopping me on the nose.

"So, what are you saying? That it all happened like, like it was planned? Like what, it's all predestined?"

"I don't know about that stuff. Maybe your dad does, I dunno. All I know is that I'm getting these visions from somewhere, and this is how they work. I trust them."

"Yeah, Ang," David said. "Just like we trust each other, and it all works out. I figure," he mused, twisting the twist tie from the bag of pretzels into a little ball, "sometimes the less you worry about stuff, the better it works out."

I stared at him. "Don't overthink?"

"Right!"

"And don't worry?"

"Right!"

"But David, those are like, my two best things!" I complained.

Jen looked at me then, her big green eyes twinkling. "That's not what Jon thinks," she said, coyly.

David guffawed.

"WHAT? No, wait, WHAT??"

David crowed with laughter. I turned beet red, my head snapping back and forth between the two of them, mouth hanging open. Jen was grinning like a loon, and David was rolling around, kicking his feet in the air.

"Honestly, Brainiac. You're just now figuring this out?" he demanded. "Jeez! Jon's been gaga over you since, since forever!"

"WHAT?!? How do I not know any of this??" I cried.

Jen chuckled. "He's pretty low key if you hadn't noticed. He's always played it cool because he was afraid it would totally freak you out," she said, looking at me pointedly.

Well, he was right about that, I thought.

"And you know," she continued. "We've had a lot going on, with all the battling evil and whatnot."

That's when David started chanting, "Jon and Angie, sitting in a tree, K-I-S-S-I-N-G."

Jen and I both started pelting him with pillows from the couch. The full-scale pillow fight that ensued was raucous, mildly destructive, and quite therapeutic. Once we finally stopped, spent, and eyed the overturned card table that had spilled several games and at least one puzzle onto the floor, I felt much clearer headed. For a minute or two, anyway.

"So, what are we supposed to do now? I asked. "How is this supposed to work? Isn't everything going to be weird and awkward? What if he . . . if we . . .” I trailed off, the word ‘we’ sticking in my mouth like unexpectedly sweet candy.

“Oh, I totally know what’s next,” Jen snickered, reaching for my hair and pulling me back over to the couch so she could braid it.

“Oh, yeah. It’s the next logical step,” David agreed.

“What the heck are you guys even talking about?” I demanded.

“Next weekend, right?” David asked Jen.

“Yep!” she replied.

“WHAT??” I yelled.

As one, in an utterly delighted tone that gave me goosebumps of horrific anticipation, they shouted, “Rec Center Dance!”

I covered my face with both hands. Heaven help me.

Note from the Author

The murder case referenced in this story is true. Mary O'Shea was assaulted, raped and murdered in her home in Lincoln in September of 1966. Two young children were home at the time. One of them provided eyewitness information.

Her killer was quickly found and arrested. He was charged with first degree murder, found guilty and sentenced to the death penalty. His sentence was later commuted to life in prison.

Everything else in the story is a work of fiction.

Beck, Margery. "Jury Weighing Death Penalty After 3 Decades." Yankton Daily Press & Dakotan, 11 Sept. 2003.

Gaughan, Clement, and Richard L Goos. "State v. Alvarez 154 N.W.2d 746 (1967) 182 Neb. 358. STATE of Nebraska, Appellee, v. Thomas A. ALVAREZ, Appellant. No. 36637. Supreme Court of Nebraska. December 8, 1967." Justia.com, 2019, law.justia.com/cases/nebraska/supreme-court/1967/36637-1.html.

About the Author

Sarah Dale is an author, mom, partner, daughter, step-mom, friend, dog-walker, cat-appreciator, library book-balancer, word lover, think-thinker and picture-taker living in Lincoln, Nebraska, and just generally trying to get things done.

www.sarahdaleauthor.com

Facebook: facebook.com/wecouldbeheroesnovel/

Twitter: @sarahdaleauthor

Instagram: instagram.com/wecouldbeheroesnovel/

Goodreads: goodreads.com/stillphoenix

Amazon: amazon.com/author/stillphoenix

Other titles you might enjoy from Snowy Wings Publishing

Sand and Snow
-Janina Franck

Copper Mage
-Dorothy Dreyer

Between Worlds
-Micky O'Brady

Look for these and more at
www.snowywingspublishing.com/books

9 781948 661881